The Bromsgrove Collectors' Society

'A Murder in the Midst'

The Bromsgrove Collectors' Society

'A Murder in the Midst'

Steven George

First Edition 2024

ISBN 979-88826223-5-9

Contents

This book is dedicated to my wife and soul mate Sharon,
my beautiful children Daniel and Grace,
their wonderful partners Kerry-Ann and Nitin
and our joyful grandchildren to date, Siena Rose and Sofia.
They have all brought me love, happiness and contentment
and I am lucky to have them in my life.

Characters

There are twelve characters in this book. All are protagonists in their own right. Please get to know them well dear reader, as you may need to formulate a judgement of your own from what I am about to tell you.

The triplets. Listed below. *Together, they collect vintage designer handbags and perfume bottles.* They were born in nineteen-ninety-two and have just turned thirty years old. Off spring of a now deceased mother who died during childbirth and an eccentric writer father who named them all on the basis of his favourite tastes and his acquired infatuation on the flavours in oranges, liquorice, vanilla and caramel. He raised them alone with the support of his sister-in-law, 7 below. The girls inherited the family home in Hanbury where they continue to live together and from where they run a joint business venture. An apparent united front by the sisters hide underlying issues on their relationships arising from petty jealousies. They all have long standing knowledge of 4 5 and 6 as all six had been day scholars at Bromsgrove Independent School.

1. **Sassy** (Sarsaparilla) **Cartwright** . Thirty years old. The eldest and most attractive of the Cartwright sisters; she is the tallest at five feet nine inches. Strawberry blond probably from her mother's side (nee Macdonald). Strong personal presence with green eyes, a pale complexion and a wide endearing smile that petals her mouth to show a wonderfully perfect set of white teeth. She cares the least of her sisters about personal appearance but most about personal health. Can be seen out in jeans and a T-shirt or gym kit during the day. Dressing up involves designer blouses with darker jeans but she does recognise a formal occasion when required and is impressive in a long dress.

2. **Clemmie** (Clementine) **Cartwright.** Thirty years old. The middle one. Arguably the most thoughtful but certainly the hardest working. She is five feet eight inches and is the broadest of the girls in stature. Darker in complexion and carrying a mane of light brown hair and matching hazel eyes she highlights her hair and makes up to match. She dresses smartly in shift

dresses and shops in the higher end high street stores and concessions.

3. **Ora** (Liquorice) **Cartwright**. Thirty years old. She is the youngest and shortest of the sisters measuring five feet seven and a half inches. She is bubbly and very active. She has blond hair and blue eyes and resents a stereotypically view as being known for her 'blonde absent minded ways', due to her propensity to pick up part of a story and run with it and get the 'wrong end of the stick'. She is rounded nose and a small scar on her right cheek from an old hockey injury gives her a unique attractiveness.

4. **Maximilian Charles**. Thirty-three years old. *Has a modest collection of classic cars consisting of a Morgan, a Midget, a Royale Sabre and a Maserati GranTurismo.* Six feet two inches tall and weighs two hundred and two pounds. Rugby player with slim hips and broad shoulders. Roman nose and narrow jaw with a mop of long thick blond hair that he habitually brushes back between his fingers. Dresses in a shirt and tie for most occasions, he covers it with a tradesman's boiler suit when he's playing with his cars. He carries a pompous air bordering on arrogance but he doesn't

see himself as privileged. His private school education helps cement his image. Lives off an allowance, is not too motivated about earning money and relies on his parents to supplement his income. Originally from Worcester before moving to Chaddesley Corbett upon leaving home. Outspoken and opinionated, he sees himself above the crowd and does not hide a dislike for social aspirants. Loves dating women but at the same time doesn't hold them in high esteem. Sometimes openly hostile and seeks to belittle given the opportunity. Widely appreciated and disliked in equal measure amongst friends and acquaintances.

5. **Lickey Farrier**. Twenty-nine years old. *Collector of jewellery*. Five feet seven inches tall. Long straight blond hair and gentle light blue eyes. Delicate frame bordering on medically undernourished suggesting a need to control. Named after the hills where she grew up. Loves dressing in outfits with a floral romantic English design which, unless it is very warm, she complements with a petit cashmere cardigan in various colours. She is the daughter of a self-made man from the Black Country who owned a large successful fencing business. Based in a sizable property in the well to do Barnt Green area.

6. **Bartholomew Bramble**. Thirty-seven years old. *Football programme and signature collector.* A graduate of Durham University where he studied Philosophy Politics and Economics, he returned to the town of his birth to pursue a political career. This has frustratingly evaded him at the ballot box. Despite years on the football terrace and his obvious intelligence and opportunity he has come to recognise that he does not have the personal touch required to cement a political following despite the support and coaching of 7. He blames 'backing the wrong political horse' for his failure. Now lives in a cottage on Grafton Lane.

7. **Elise Goodrich**. Sixty-one years old. *Holds a handsome collection of vintage designer handbags. Also collects obsolete and current currency and dabbles in crypto.* Reputedly a wealthy widow held in high esteem in the community. Her late husband became the local MP after a successful career in the civil service. Now has almost entirely grey hair that yet still frames a healthy complexion, she spends much of her time at home and ventures out to events and activities that keep her mind alert. She enjoys hosting visitors and is a skilful raconteur. Lives on the prosperous College Road a short stroll down a narrow walkway to the town high street.

8. **Lamont Adams.** Thirty-five years old. *Collects vinyl single and long- playing records.* Six feet and three inches tall with brown eyes and a square jaw he weighs in at two hundred and sixteen pounds. Wears his hair very short and clean to the scalp. Shaped like an Adonis and muscles in keeping. An ethnically black sports and personal fitness instructor. Works from his home in Churchfields area not far from St John's church and the town's cemetery.

9. **Sangita** (Divine Music) **Kumari** (Goddess, Princess) **Sangar**. Fifty years old. *Collects art work and a developing interest in Bitcoin.* Short in stature at five foot four with dark hair and brown eyes. Occasionally wears traditional Indian dress but at other times adopts a western appearance. She is an Art Blogger and columnist living in Burcot. There are unsubstantiated rumours around her involvement in handling counterfeit art work and hiding the proceeds in bit coin.

10. **Balwinder** (Powerful King) **Singh** (Lion). Forty-six years old. *Collects old letters and filmscripts as well as gathering old artifacts from the Punjab.* Six feet tall exactly but appears taller when wearing a turban. Lean, long limbed in appearance with an ambling gait. His

extraordinary flexibility has led to him becoming the local yoga guru. Lives and practices in the Stoney Hill area of town.

11. **Detective Inspector (DI) Raymond Chandler**. Forty-eight years old. *Takes pride in collecting nothing but criminals*. Five feet and eleven inches tall with excellent posture he cuts a commanding figure. Wears a white shirt and tie together with a three-piece suit and has a penchant for quality branded shoes. Regularly wears varifocal glasses when investigating. Classic neat cut dark blond hairstyle with a slight quiff off a parting left to right. Regular use of men's fragrance and naturally inquisitive and excellent investigator. A vastly experience officer of the West Mercian force. Moved into the Criminal Investigation Department (CID) when he was found to have all the essential strengths in enquiry, interviewing and investigation.

12. **Andrew Byron**. I am thirty-nine years old, the narrator and associate to all. I *collect stamps* and am deeply attached to the town and widely networked into it. At five feet and nine inches tall I am not ashamed to admit I am little overweight at one hundred and eighty pounds. I do not think I carry the same presence of some

of my counterparts but try to make up for it through my interest in people, my sociability and my intellectual pursuits. I consider myself to have sufficient gravitas to illicit trust and confidence.

1. The Idea. 10th October 2022. (Before)

The spire of St John the Baptist Church stretches magnificently high into the skyline above the market town of Bromsgrove in Worcestershire. It looks down in all directions on Worcester to the south, Kidderminster to the west, Redditch to the east and the busy bustling centre of Bromsgrove to the immediate north and on up to the Lickey Hills. Built of red sandstone in the fourteenth century, the church has watched over many life events of local parishioners of all denominations and persuasions. It has been rained on by the tears of dissolution and reformation, felt the sun burn at birth of empire and observed the fog of war. It has danced with Luftwaffe flying over to more important strategic targets and its bells have sung with victory and chimed with many Kings and Queens across the ages. It has also from time to time born witness to celebration and joy coupled with conspiracy and deceit among its own ministry.

My name is Andrew Byron and I occupy many of my daylight hours acting as a legal clerk for a family firm of solicitors run by David Fairly and Sean Good working out of offices that occupy the Churchfields district of the town. At certain parts of the day, I regularly sit in the shadow of St John's. From my rather small yet splendidly appointed window of my Fairly Good office I can see much of the town bustling by day with the business of folk and the chatter of family. This is my story and like my days it will cast shadow and light on my home town. It is played out in this apparently rather indistinguishable and unremarkable backwater of central England. You will discover, like me, all is not as it seems. It is not a story that I tell without some regret for my part in its denouement and climax and it is one that is no less thrilling and traumatic that those significant events of the past mentioned above. The impact and consequences on those whose lives I am about to unfold is calculable only by the degree of happiness, enlightenment, pain or suffering felt by all in this story……..

In some ways I suppose this tale of human strength and frailty started in the Queens Head public house and restaurant. This popular hostelry sits on the bank of the Birmingham to Worcester canal about three miles from Bromsgrove centre; (in reality you will come to realise that this story started much earlier). I thought it apposite to be there for what I was intending to propose to my friends. It was seven pm. The three of us were perched on bar stools gathered round an old barrel table. The table was dressed with a solitary candle which flickered a spirited light across our faces making us look like three wise men addressing the magi. The only clue to the canal that ran alongside our window was the moonlight that bounced off the still water through the large panes of glass.

'It is certainly self-evident to me that everyman should hold a collection of some sort' said Lamont Adams, 'It is not only a rite of passage and a nod to the past but also displays a wider appreciation of history. The Victorians were insightful as seeing childhood hobbies as important. They foster interest, develop knowledge, create a love of learning and give meaning to the sometimes mundane.'

'I agree,' I replied. 'There is no doubt that my appreciation of the world both historical and geographical has been aided by my philatelic interests.'

'We can certainly learn from each other through our collections, you with your postage stamps, Lamont with his esoteric collection of vinyl classics and me with my keen interest in all things 'motor car'. My love of classic car designs informs and widens my understanding of how we arrive at where we are. I do not however, have any idea how we could link these interests together!' Maximillian Charles broke into a wide grin that stretched across his chiselled chin as he stood to stretch his long muscular legs. 'Vinyl records and classic cars don't have a lot in common. A bit like Lamont and I,' he mused as he gathered the glasses and strode to the bar for another round of drinks.

I could not help envying his striking looks, reminiscent of a Viking Norseman with wild blonde hair, broad shoulders, a strong chin softened by a short layer of stubble and a broad chest that narrowed into a healthy waistline. He wore a designer shirt and a pair of casual trousers, both a little too bright to blend into the background. It was true to say that Max was never one to blend into the background.

Lamont turned his head away and lifted his square jaw with an air of contempt. An air that was not new. They were very hard work together but it didn't put me off. I reckoned on the friction between them to produce unforeseen benefit. I liked both men separately and they were both good friends with me if not each other. Although they had arrived in the present from very different places I figured that they were both too similar and too full of testosterone to get along. Every sentence one said was interpreted like a that a challenge to the other. Papering over Lamont's apparent disdain I tried to address Max's concern.

'You're right Max but do we need to have a link? They're very different entities and it would be interesting to discover how our motives drive our passions whilst giving an opportunity to spread our own evangelical messages,' I said. 'Collecting can be a little like music. It needs plenty of practice but then is at its best with an appreciative audience.' My look of thoughtful reflection was not lost on my company. Composure returned to Lamont's face and Max was not slow in responding.

'If it is a society you're looking for then a club of three is no club at all my friend. We'd have to include others. We could make it invitation only. I was talking to Balwinder Gupta after yoga class the other day and he was telling me about how much time he spends on his collection of scripts from film and other cartographical works. He may only have a relatively small collection but he is immensely proud of it! What he knows about his beloved writings though was very interesting.'

'Yes, and I know the triplets would be good value with their collection of high-end handbags and perfume bottles. That would make seven if they are all keen to join us,' interjected Lamont.

The triplets as they were affectionately known, were the daughters of the formerly eccentric writer but now deceased father, Julian Cartwright. He named the girls on the basis of his infatuation with his favourite tastes and flavours of oranges, liquorice, vanilla and caramel. The daughters lived together in their inherited family home on the lane leading to Hanbury Hall where they have continued to live together to the present day. These lovely women suffered early tragedy when their mother died during childbirth. As well as losing their mother, the chances of fraternal triplets being small (one in ten thousand pregnancies) and the chances of them being all girls was also small (about twelve percent), the girls were treasured by their father and they grew up knowing that they were loved and lacked for nothing. Julian adored their individuality both in their looks and in their outlooks and taught them to embrace their differences. Sarsaparilla (Sassy) Cartwright was the eldest and probably the most attractive of the triplets and certainly the tallest at five feet ten inches. She wore her strawberry blond hair up in a bun unless evening dress etiquette favoured on it being worn over her shoulders. Her colouring probably from her mother's side (nee Macdonald). She had a strong personal presence and her piercing green eyes and a pale complexion were magnetic. Clementine (Clemmie) Cartwright was the middle one. Arguably the cleverest but certainly the hardest working. She was five feet and eight inches and was the broadest of the girls. Her complexion reflected an interest spending her time outdoors and although her hair was a natural brown she lifted her colouring though carefully coiffured highlights and make up to match. Her wit and intelligence shone through her hazel brown eyes that drew me towards her as my favourite of the three lovely women. Last but not least Liquorice (Ora) Cartwright was the youngest by a few minutes and shortest by half an inch of the sisters measuring five feet seven and a half inches. She constantly bubbled and was incessantly active. Ora had blond hair, blue eyes and a button nose and thus became known as the 'looker' of the girls. Fittingly and in keeping with reputation she was also the most 'dippy' of them; a reputation that she resented and challenged regularly. She favoured pink in most of her clothing. When the clothes were another colour, she accessorizes in pink. All three of these sisters, I knew, made very good company.

'That could constitute a starting quorum I think.' I sat back on my stool with a satisfied smile to ponder this development. My idea of a collectors society had taken a breath of life although it was a long way from sustaining itself just yet. 'Seven would be magnificent' I said gaining further satisfaction from my link to an old famous film 'but I would feel happier with a round ten to start a group. That number would allow for absentees on any given day. You all must appreciate how difficult it is to align times and dates and we don't even know if all of the people we mentioned will respond positively.' I stopped for thought and let the buzz of the background noise wash over me. 'What about Lickey Farrier, she loves her jewellery, is proud to wear it and I always find her quietly articulate?'

Lamont voiced his agreement but Max remained silent and just nodded in apparent quiet acceptance. We were both aware that Max and Lickey could be explosive together. He could be an awkward, irritating individual and she a delicate soul sensitive to criticism. She was a young collector but had amassed a serious amount of jewellery for a twenty- nine- year-old woman. Her knowledge on the subject was keen and no one would challenge that her interest was genuine, with period pieces forming the bulk of her holding. I knew that these two were also not an easy social match and Max was a common agent provocateur. Maybe that's why Lamont suggested her but again I was not going to let that fact detract from a potential positive to the group as a whole. 'Well, that's eight; any others we know?

'What about Elise Goodrich? It would be fitting to bring her into the fold considering her family link and influence on the triplets,' suggested Max.

It had been Elise who had advised their father to moderate the naming of the girls and had managed to convince him that the abbreviated names Sassy, Clemmie and Ora would benefit them as they grew up and avoid ridicule. Even though they loved their father they were ever thankful to her for her counsel. From the depths of his despair he had taken the advice from his sister-in-law and happily the girls had grown up loving their names.

Max continued.

'She's also a stalwart figure of the town and a court leet member. I know she's more senior in age to most of those mentioned but she certainly has her faculties about her. Her expertise in old coins is formidable and did you know she is dabbling into the crypto currency market? She may be approaching senior citizenship but she's not living in the past.'

Elise was very much a senior citizen. At sixty-one years old she may not have been as spritely as some but she looked after herself and her mind was still very bright. Her knowledge of old coinage and more surprisingly crypto currency was enlightening. It was her friendship with Balwinder that had brought her to our attention as they were quite close neighbours. Balwinder has taken on a watching brief with Elise as she now lived alone after her husband, a local MP for Bromsgrove, had suddenly passed away of a heart attack eighteen months ago. Max, Lamont and Elise all shared an interest in the local court leet.

'I like it Max; Elise would be a good contributor. She is very socially astute and has quite a social network. If there was room for growth in the future we could rely on her.'

Lamont rubbed his broad square chin. 'I have a suggestion for the round ten you seek,' he said. 'It sort of links with Elise actually and you may know her as she and her are good friends. You may know Sangita Sangar as a pharmacist owner in town but she is also an arts blogger working from home in the Burcot area and is a curator of various art work. Like all the best collectors she collects what she likes. I could check her out. She too has invested in crypto although I'm not sure that counts as a collecting thing.'

'Who knows where that sits in the world order just yet,' I said. 'It isn't a tangible thing and collectors tend to appreciate tangible things. It's probably not relevant to us but the inclusion of art in our little club would be thrilling. Yes, I know Sangita. I did her conveyancing work on her house a few years ago and she drops. Excellent! We have a group of ten. If our society gets off the runway, we may find it flies diversely and exponentially along various routes! I think that we should congratulate ourselves on a plan. All we have to do now is activate it. My round I think.' I strode to the bar with a confident spring in my step with the knowledge that I had set in motion an idea that had been swimming around my head for some time. 'Three pints of golden please barman,' I said, knowing that this would be our last and thankful for the taxi we had ordered to transport us all home.

And so, this story began at these tentative beginnings and worked its way through to its extraordinary end.

2. The Gathering.
24th October 2022. (Before)

The stage was set. Arranging a date and bringing people together had been no mean feat but I had managed to hire part of the Guesten Hall on the grounds of Avoncroft Museum at a very reasonable price that I had been happy to cover for the first event. I was keen to host the first meeting there since the building itself was part of a collection of buildings saved from demolition or neglect by the proprietors of this excellent outdoor museum. It housed among other things a mission church from 1891, an Anderson bomb shelter from the 1940's and an 1820 Windmill of a post design. The Hall itself was built in the fourteenth century by Prior Wulstan de Bransford. Its roof was originally on Worcester Cathedral's reception hall for guests and the museum had managed to preserve the impressive details of medieval carpentry. While the hall was too big for our small group, we had occupied an upper space in the building called the Weavers Gallery, more suited for the size of our gathering.

Each participant had their own presentation desk all with carefully crafted displays of their areas of interest. I had asked each contributor to bring a bottle of their favourite tipple to lubricate the works and get the tongues wagging. As I watched each stall take shape I did wonder if that had been a necessary request since there was much relaxed chatter and excited dialogue. There was certainly colour and variety in the displays guarded by proud owners. As she sipped her martini cocktail from a plastic cup Elise was teasing me. 'Come on Andrew', she said. 'What is the common denominator in the room? Just what is it that makes a collector a collector? What is the common mission if there is one and what are their aims and the purposes?'

'The collector is a breed Elise,' I replied. 'They all seek the same satisfaction as guardians of history in whatever field they choose to collect. They seek perfection. They are appreciative of value, of course, and seek to curate and archive their knowledge and understanding. They take pleasure in securing the past and wonder at emblems of the future. I think the commonality across all collectors lies, on the one hand, in the enjoyment of collecting beautiful and interesting things whilst on the other, accepting the challenge in the search for quality and rarity.'

I lifted my eyes to scan the room and saw Max in his element deep in conversation with Lickey Farrier. She was more than holding her own I noticed. He had brought the 1996 2.4 V6 Royale Sabre two-seater convertible. It was stunning in dark blue that contracted elegantly with the cream upholstery. He loved the drama of being noticed on arrival but was working hard to help visualise his prestige cars in a room such as this. He talked a good game and had brought photographs of his cars and laid them our carefully on his table to share with interested parties. I once asked him how he had chosen the cars in his possession. He replied that there was no rhyme or reason other than the fact that he liked them better than the other ones around and available. He was a great example of a collector who collected things that he liked. An important footnote to collecting, I recalled at the time and one that all collectors should refer to when adding to their stock.

Catching Elise's undeterred eye we shared a knowing smile and I continued.

'You can learn so much about the world. The philatelist protects a piece of time and is excited by the things to come. Take British stamps for example. Without

15

wishing to state the obvious, higher value stamps retain higher values. Stamp values vary according to age, often the older the better but then not always; used or unused? again often unused stamps – but sometimes used – hold the greater value; the collector seeks perfection but imperfections such as mistakes in the printing process called errors often add value due to the rarity; perforations and plate number in for example Victorian stamps are important.'

I paused again to allow Elise to break the conversation but she showed no signs of disengagement. I didn't want to be become tedious to any of my guests nor hold on to them too long when they had their own interests to share. There was no sign that put me off.

'The penny black is famous but the wrong one can be dwarfed in value by the right two penny blue. A pristine unused example of a plate one, one shilling brown with the right watermark can fetch two hundred thousand pounds while an example of a one penny used plate seventy-seven lists at six hundred thousand pounds plus.' I took a breath. 'Then there is what is in vogue. There was a time when first day covers were the things to collect but these have a smaller re-sale value now thanks to the post office and large-scale interest. Better to collect presentation packs or mint sets and gutter 'traffic light' pairs that all, generally, do better. Full sets can do better than individual stamps. Whilst the value of any collection should be monitored primarily for insurance purposes, collectors understand that the value of their collection can go up and down just like any other commodity. The intrinsic value lies in the interest and pleasure that the collection brings. More than all of this, stamps are excellent social and political history. Do I need to go on or am I boring you?' I asked politely.

'No, not at all. I love the enthusiasm that arises from a cause. I only seek to understand it more.' She lifted her head from the display. I await to share your gutter traffic light pairs,' she said playfully as she moved effortlessly on to her next unwitting prey. Bartholomew filled the vacuum, smiling as he drifted into her space.

'She got you then?'

'She's a clever lady and yet despite her age is as sharp as ever,' I said musingly yet thinking out loud. I recognised Bartholomew Bramble next to me. 'I wasn't expecting you,' I said probably too abruptly. He was tall with a loping gait, which I knew he put to good use in his want for long distance road running. He had attractive facial features with dark hair and soft brown eyes and had adopted slightly rounding shoulders over time, which I interpreted as an attempt to compensate for his height in company. He was recognised as a 'good egg' around the town. Connecting with the present again I felt sure Bart did not feature in the names discussed at the Queens Head. 'It appears so, although I feel I was able to hold my own under her gaze,' I said changing the subject.

'Good for you,' he replied and in recognition of my unthinking slight went on, 'Yes, I sort of tagged along with Sangita. She's a good friend and she thought it would be good for me to get out more and see something a bit different. She told me about the invite and said she didn't think you'd mind. I was also attracted when Max told me he was bringing the V6 Royale Sabre convertible. He hardly ever takes that car out so it was a good opportunity to view it. I see you have pulled a few strings to get it parked outside. Well done. Look, I brought this as an offering'.

A bottle of wine. Not hers and not his to decide I thought. A call would have been nice. It wasn't his presence but it was the assumption that I wasn't keen on.. Anyway, one more didn't make too much difference. I hope I disguised my feelings well enough as I continued, 'Not a problem, make yourself at home. Have you brought anything to show?'

'Well actually no. I thought I would browse and show interest and get the lay of the land. See if it might spark an old flame you know'.

I smiled inanely. No, I didn't know I thought and I didn't much care. Not that I could do anything without causing an unseemly scene and any scene that could happen was not going to have me in it. I wanted this evening to be a success and a prelude to more.

Bart filled the moment of awkward silence and I was glad of it. 'I've known her a long time and love her company but Elize really only understands money and has little appreciation of older things even though she is one herself. Once the gloss has been wiped off it becomes disposable. I think she refreshes to refresh herself. Not very PC I'm afraid. She's not one for recycling. One must give her credit for embracing crypto at her age. She's still driven by personal growth which is highly commendable given her advancing years.

I had no idea what he was talking about.

'Having said that, she will graciously hold her own if you mention her coin collection.'

We both glanced over in her direction. She had picked up something from her table and was holding Ora's avid attention.

'She told me once that she was a numismatist and I thought she worked a piece of factory machinery in the Black Country,' Bart continued 'but it turned out nomisma is a Greek word for coin so that's how it became the collective noun. Bit boring I know but that's our Elise.

Another social gaff but he wouldn't have recognised it. I was always surprised by people and their propensity to share their thoughts without thinking of their impact. Some call it brave and forthright but I called it insensitive and inconsiderate. I defended Elise politely with my reply and tried to steer the conversation. I found him hard work but Elise had always been patient and kind to him especially during his failed flirtations into local politics.

'To be fair to her Bartholomew, after all the hype and expressions of love towards our interests and our most vocal laudable aims, the conversations invariably turn to value and money as the key. That's what impresses the public in general although the collector likes to think he or she has a higher calling. The purists amongst us may have some reservations about sharing current worth and price. We think that it reflects a knowing the price of everything and the value of nothing. Collectors, just like everyone else, seek to keep abreast of trends and don't like going down rabbit holes. Our meetings could become a special variegated edition of the BBC's Antiques Roadshow if we don't stay true to our art!'

I could see him losing interest and but I did not relent. Punishing him for his rudeness towards Elise I continued to make him listen.

'Look at Lamont over there showing samples of his album covers from the later part of the twentieth century. He'll be dissecting the art work from Jimmy Hendricks '*Are You Experienced*', the Rolling Stones '*Sticky Fingers*' or David Bowie's '*Aladdin Sane*'. Then he'll be drooling over the Beatles '*Sergeant Pepper's* or Bob Marley's '*Exodus*' and discussing the relative merits of Led Zeppelin's '*Houses of the Holy*' and Pink Floyd's '*Dark Side of the Moon*'. The list goes on. He will be in mid-point ecstasy and eulogy then someone will ask him the price of one and although he'd rather not express the value of the art and the priceless artifact he'll still come up with a figure! Go and try my theory out. We glanced over together. Bartholomew smiled, politely this time, sharing the sentiment and took a sip of his, what I thought looked like, a rather thin and insipid looking red wine. If he didn't like the taste he hid it well.

Lamont set a striking image. Tall, lean and strong. Every bit the personal fitness instructor that he was with classic close cut Caribbean features and an engaging smile to boot. He had first met Elise at the constituency offices where she was supporting her husband at his surgery. Lamont had grown up with strong values and a work ethic that had helped him cement his political views. They had hit it off straight away and found they shared a similar philosophy of life, living the best life available at the time whilst striving to improve though endeavour.

With the formalities and greetings having been completed around the room, members of this most unusual club were relaxing into their subjects and finding their voices. I was pleased in my efforts to persuade them to attend. They all had so much to offer each other and the local community with their knowledge and history in so many different areas. Here was a tentative exploration to reinvigorate the towns museum and fill it with artifacts sourced locally and internationally. I was beginning to inwardly smile at my success so far, when I heard an argument appearing to be gathering some heat.

'Don't tell me anymore. That story is not true and you mustn't spread it.' The voice clearly belonged to Lickey Farrier. 'My father was the most honest and decent of men and had to learn to deal with his acquired wealth unlike some in this room. He wasn't handed a silver spoon or in your case a pompous ass.'

The hairs stood up on the back of my neck. I instinctively knew Max would be involved. I had helped him out of so many scrapes as he had grown up that I had lost count. I looked across towards him and he was grinning triumphantly as one who had knowingly stoked a fire and successfully fanned the flames. In a voice that carried too much volume for the occasion he came back at Lickey like a steam train.

'You know it's true, your father lacked the class and intellectual capacity to build a solid reputation. He put up sub-standard wooden garden fences for far too much money. He wasn't honest in his dealings with people and sold weak larch lap products to unwitting dimwits. You must be proud. You can dress it how you like but the testimony of his customers on trust pilot cannot be denied'.

Lickey's swimming pool blue eyes began to leak with distress. Her pale cheeks were burning crimson and her chest rose and fell with short breaths of angry hue. I had invited her and she had accepted in good faith to share her love of jewellery and was faced with this often buffoon of a man intent on goading her as he did with so many. She hated him when he was like this. Bartholomew looked stunned and his face reddened, his body frozen as he stared at his feet. A strange reaction I thought. Leaving him to fend for himself, I walked quickly but without undue haste in her direction and held a supportive hand to her elbow. Saying a gritted 'excuse me' that left Max knowing very clearly how I felt about him I led her away with any inane words I could muster to deflect the conversation. 'Thank you for coming tonight, Lickey. Show me your delicious jewellery that you have brought with you to show.'

'I am so angry with him Andrew,' she hissed through tense lips. 'One minute he is flatteringly kind and considerate and the next he insults my family. I haven't the words to describe how much I detest him right now.'

'Everyone knows he's attractive and interesting but that doesn't trump his over privileged idiocy,' I said interjecting hastily. 'Don't rise to his occasion. I think he does it on purpose. Look at him, he either relishes being a social time bomb or is totally unaware. Sometimes I think it's both but ultimately it's the attention he seeks. That's his real weakness. I'm sorry you had to suffer that exchange.' I was upset and angry about the effect on the evening but I needn't have worried.

'You're too kind Andrew, don't worry about me,' she replied regaining her composure. 'You forgive and look for the best of people. That's your strength.' She gave me a light kiss on the cheek.

Maximillian had already moved on to another conversation with ease holding a wide grin across his face and was oblivious to the offence he had caused. Heads that had turned had been satisfied and spun back to re-join their own discussions.

'Oh, how he always succeeds at winding me up. It isn't even that I don't like him but he is such a snob and how dare he insult me through my father in public. He has no right you know. My father was a good man and I don't understand why he behaves so.'

'I think it's his own insecurities Lickey. He is not like that all the time and I think he sniffs out weakness like a bully. Be strong with him and remain aloof. He won't like that. Don't rise to the bait.'

25

Lickey fumbled in her handbag to draw out a delightfully necklace of rolled gold inset with what looked like a very bright cushion cut diamond pendant of, I guessed, approximately one and a half carat. The sight of it immediately altered her expression and lightened her features. It had been packaged in a sealed plastic wallet and she spent a few seconds separating it from what she told me was a Bulgari Rose Gold diamond Serpanti Seduttori ring. It seemed a clumsy method of transport for such lovely jewellery but she obviously loved it together with what looked like an older piece. They both served to distract her from her recent conversation.

'This was my grandmother's Andrew,' she said gently placing the ring on her finger and casting the chain over her forearm so that the diamond had prominence. It is not the most expensive piece I have but it is one of my most treasured. I thought people would like to see it.'

I examined it recognising it's beauty and style. It certainly looked like a high-grade diamond with no obvious flaws or blemishes to the naked eye. It was beautifully bright and the facets lined up well. That was the extent of my expertise and I could see why Lickey loved the piece not just for the look but also for the family history. Collectors often had a weak spot for generational heir looms. To be honest I liked the ring better.

Attracted by the light, others recognised their interest and were draw into her orbit. Having hoped to have calmed those waters at least temporarily, the heat in the room subsided and a more even temperate climate prevailed. The enthusiastic murmur of focused interest had returned to the room.

'What do you call a group of collectors Andrew?' It was Ora chased by her two shadows Clemmie and Sassy. 'I think maybe a set of or a provenance of… or perhaps a comedy of ….' she laughed turning round to seek approval from her sisters.

'Oh no,' retorted Clemmie appearing to come to my rescue, 'those names are not grand enough. I would classify a collector alongside the musical conductor who brings together the strings, the percussion and the wind to form an orchestra. Why, they are symphonic …. they are a symphony… a symphony of collectors!'

I think I may have blushed as my affection for Clemmie was not a deep secret. I l looked directly into her piercing brown eyes.

'I rather like that, Clemmie. Very nicely put and although your tone is frivolous, I like the suggestion. The pleasure for the collector builds slowly and in stages building to a crescendo as a piece or pieces fall into place. There is a musical synonym there somewhere. You may have mistakenly or inadvertently given us all a name in your teasing.'

Smiles all round. This is going very well at last I thought. A symphony of collectors all playing their own tunes.

'Sorry Andrew,' Sassy broke my silent contemplation. 'I'm not putting this down anywhere even though I trust your invitees. This is an old Gucci Horsebit bag from the 1970's. It was one that Aunt Elise gave me so has a special place for me'

Not to be outdone Ora held out her hand. 'And this Andrew is my Paco Rabanne chainmail from 1969. It actually only usually comes out after nineteen hundred hours so you're lucky to see it'.

Clemmie was more reserved. 'I bet you wish you'd never asked,' she said.

'I didn't know I had,' I replied.

Chuckles all round.

While I've got you three here,' I went on, 'have any of you got any ideas where we might go from here? I would be interested to listen to your thoughts.'

The sisters looked at each other as if in some sort of telepathic trance. Clemmie was first to speak. I was glad. I always thought I got most sense from her.

'Well we were chatting earlier with Aunt Elise and we all thought it would be nice to open up an evening like this to anyone who wanted to come; like an open forum where people could ask questions and view objects. Collectors of all persuasions might be interested.'

'That's a good idea Clemmie although I would worry about people that I don't know entering a room full of precious items that may have monetary as well as intrinsic value. We would have to ensure safety and that would push security for such a gathering to another level.'

'Well I wouldn't want to put you to any additional stress Andrew. We just thought it might be a good idea.'

'Oh yes, yes.... yes it is Clemmie. I was just thinking out aloud,' I said quick to point out my appreciation of her ideas.

We spent some time on the skeleton of an evening. Thinking back it was probably more than that with all the meat and bones added by my very willing assistants. They left me with very little further thinking to do, with only the task of arranging it down to me.

I recall thinking if I ever ask for ideas from the sisters again I'll be prepared with a pen and paper.

'A symphony of collectors all playing their own tunes' I repeated to myself. As it turned out it should have been a murder of crows.

3. The Shock.
13th November 2022 (Ground Zero)

Balwinder had invited me round to his home for a relaxing evening with a few male friends. I accepted graciously and had joined Max and Bart in the enjoyable bonhomie.

'Do you know that a nineteen ninety-six film script for the Titanic recently sold for eight hundred pounds and the nineteen ninety-eight Start Trek Voyager script sold for six hundred and fifty pounds around the same time? Now what wonderful things could you collect that are so interesting to read? Having seen both these films and thoroughly enjoyed viewing them I would be proud to own them.' Balwinder preened before he became aware of his loftiness. He needn't have worried; we were all hooked. He carried on.

'I have come to understand that because movies may be in development for many years, with a variety of different writers and directors attached to them. One script can be very different in its content from another and this creates its own uniqueness. Screenplays, some very scarce, are always prized when they appear. This demand is heightened by a signature or two. A while ago there was a West Coast auction of an original screenplay for the 1946 'The Big Sleep', signed by William Faulkner one of its writers, and it sold for about one hundred thousand pounds. Another screenplay example is an over written script by Harrison Ford for 'Raiders of the Lost Ark' changed hands for a similar amount some years ago too and were it to come to the market now it would fetch an even larger sum.'

He certainly spoke with knowledgeable surety and authority and so he should. He was probably the most prolific collector of all of us and had the most diverse portfolio. It was his moment and we owed him it. He was in possession of over one hundred film scripts of varying genres and ages. He was also a collector of letters, including in his portfolio his prize possession of Lewis Carroll's Two Original Handwritten Letters on Paper from eighteen seventy-seven, valued at a whopping nine thousand pounds. Bally also held an enviable small collection of maps and charts and numerous cultural pieces from the Punjab. He was holding court over us whilst discussing the relativity between investment over desirability and indeed, whether both were necessary for the collector.

He had been drawn into a discussion on maps describing the effect of printing methods and how they indicated a date with earlier maps using blocks or copper plate techniques. He showed us a map that he stressed was a chart and as such a more prized piece.

'… because charts were used by mariners to plot courses through open bodies of water and through busy shipping lanes,' he had said.

'So I suppose we are back to the old chest nut provenance, Bally,' I had interjected.

'Without doubt. It is more interesting to look upon any object where one can wonder about where it has been, who it belonged to and what role it played in their lives. If you gaze upon something that had helped navigate in an era of brave exploration it clearly has greater meaning.'

'Not if you're a flat earther', I teased.

The others looked on in interest to see where this was leading. Even Max remained quiet.

'Let's not go there Andrew. It's just one of the many versions of fake news that occupies our media platforms. I haven't the time or the inclination to give them my headspace.'

I couldn't help thinking that it was a good job some people did.

'At least our objectivity provided through our physical collectables help to disprove historical myths and inaccurate realities.'

I admitted that he had a good point.

Maximillian listened with the interest of the investor rather than the interest of a collector. He did not have a love for writings and he had only a small appreciation of the film genres. He pushed his fingers back though his golden mane, the evening was challenging his sensibilities yet again. Displaying a certain lack of awareness he posed a direct question.

'So, what is the appreciation of your holdings over time Bally? Take what you have held over a five-year period. Are you getting a healthy return?'

Balwinder remained polite and courteous whilst his body language signalled disapproval. 'Well, of course my appreciation lies deeper than the appreciation you request but as you ask; assuming from a date of acquisition over a five-year period you are looking at something in the range of five to ten percent. This is not the end game for me though. I have acquired a considerable benefit and enjoyment from holding and reading scripts that cannot be monetised.'

THE BROMSGROVE COLLECTORS' SOCIETY

Bartholomew smiled and sat back in his chair and stroked his chin. 'Touché,' he thought, pleased with Balwinder's riposte. He looked elegant in his black roll neck jumper, checked tweed jacket and burgundy chinos. A picture of rural life and an apparent comfortable existence.

'Good for you Bally. I heard recently that Elizabeth Taylor's hand written love letters to Richard Burton last changed hands for thirty-five thousand pounds! I think most of us know the difference between the two forms of appreciation and appreciation but fame and notoriety carry their own price.'

Max scowled but let the moment pass. He had thought about not coming this evening but he was bored at home and he had considered his attendance was the lesser of two evils.

Balwinder stretched out his long legs from beside his rather grand desk and slowly rising from his seat gestured towards a waiting and enticing whisky decanter. Well gentlemen, are we to enjoy a tipple this evening or would you prefer something else?

'Make mine a small one if it's OK with you.' I said politely.' I am enjoying the evening and don't want to spoil it with the anticipation of a thick head in the morning.'

'Here speaks the great adventurer.' mused Bartholomew.

'I doubt that very much,' I replied. 'I prefer to partake when I am celebrating not deliberating. It's easy to control then.'

My point was not universally accepted but we all accepted the invitation to take a taste of his fifteen-year-old Dalwhinnie single malt. One by one, Balwinder circulated his excellent Royal Scot Crystal tumblers with the golden nectar swaying inside the glasses.

The evening had passed agreeably enough. Discussion had wandered off the topic of collection and into people, family and friends and what they were doing and why they were doing it. It had lightened my mood. I had always enjoyed spending time with friends and Balwinder had always provided excellent company in the convivial surroundings of his three-bedroom town house in Stony Hill. Being the first to take my leave I expressed my thanks to make the short walk home. I glanced at my watch. It read ten thirty and I needed to get my head back into shape for work as I had been distracted by my enthusiasm for establishing the society. Patience is not inexhaustible I thought and good employers, whilst patient, don't wait forever. I glanced admiringly at Max's Morgan convertible as I went, smiling at his confidence to leave the top down on the street side. Typical; this was not a bad area but hey, don't tempt fate I thought. Galvanised by my actions the others were saying their good nights as I turned the corner and out of sight. I wasn't there during what followed but I've heard on good authority that the events were very close to how I have described and are hard to contest.

'Cheers for the lift Max. I realise it's a little out of your way but I do appreciate it.'

'No problem Bartholomew, that's what you do for friends and oh, don't forget the package you're picking up for me tomorrow.'

A smile drained from Bart's face and with a brief nod of reluctant acknowledgement he stepped surprisingly effortlessly from the low-lying Morgan 1987 Plus 8. It was an impressive looking car made more distinct by the Racing Green body colour, a sandy convertible roof and the beige upholstery. He took the short walk along Grafton Lane and up the drive to his converted barn overlooking the distant Malvern Hills. He felt lucky to still be able to live there. The red lights of Upton Warren radio masts that had been used for intelligence during the second world war imposed themselves upon the dark foreground like long legged sci-fi creatures. He turned to throw a half wave to Maximillian but he had already turned astutely on the narrow lane. He was negotiating the rather uneven surface up to the main road and the quickest route back to his home in Chaddesley Corbett. He was blissfully unaware of any clandestine plan being hatched against him.

Later that evening Maximillian Charles was dead in a muddy ditch on the side of the Kidderminster Road, in a tangled mess of steel, rubber and leather that used to be a Morgan 1987 Plus 8 in racing green.

4. The Work Out.
29th October 2021 (Before)

Sangita sat at her desk softly touching her finger over the mouse trying to decide whether to press or not, to twist or stick, to gamble or hold. She had not done this very often and it was a new game to her but she was getting caught up in world she did not fully understand. She was intrigued by new and emerging currency but had little experience of finance with a natural inclination towards fine art. She lived with her husband in Burcot, a small village on the outskirts of Bromsgrove, in a house whose rear garden overlooked the local golf club. She had time and space to follow her interests now that she had reduced her hours at one of the high street chemists which she and her husband had run for twenty years. He was keen to start cashing in on his investment in the pharmacy, stepping back and playing more golf. She had other ideas and was ready to take a big risk. The pharmaceutical training was a profession that her parents had been pleased to support and she had met her husband during qualification. On successfully completing their courses they both took up posts in large pharmaceutical companies and after a number of years in industry took the opportunity to purchase a clinical pharmacy business in Bromsgrove. Both families were not only delighted with their match but also the direction their careers had taken them. The families were so happy that they had bought the business so close to their Birmingham homes. They now offered status and security to their loved ones but Sangita's marriage and her career had hampered her real love of art. The pharmacy had given them both a good living and now had granted her the opportunity to do what she really wanted. She had been blogging on the subject of art for over six years, showcasing contemporary artists and publishing news and articles in trending topics. This morning she was occupied on other things. Her excursion into the crypto currency market was leaving her feeling excited yet vulnerable. 'While the cats away the mouse will play,' she whispered aloud 'and I will keep the cream to myself.'

While Sangita pondered her next financial incursion, Lamont Adams was preparing to leave for his fitness appointment at the residence of 'his Cartwright sisters' as he fondly called them. They weren't his but he loved all the of them. They were his favourite appointment and he looked forward to it as they were always full of energy, vitality and fun and very willing to make the most of their bi-weekly fitness session. Lamont prepared meticulously, carefully constructing bespoke and crafted sessions suited to client needs. That is what the girls liked about him. He didn't do generic workouts but provided thoughtful sessions after consultation. His only limitation was that he didn't have a base so those wishing to use his services had to be able to provide a facility in their own home or elsewhere. He lived comfortably in a modest Victorian semi-detached property in the central Churchfields area of the town. Good for local services and sized to suit his needs as a man who liked perfection in the home.

His family had arrived in Britain during the 1960's as part of the Windrush generation. Aspirant and hard-working they raised Lamont's parents in the same vein and the values were fed through to their grand-children. Lamont entered university and studied English with an intent to teach but found a true love in physical activity, drifting into Personal Trainer work over time. He was successful because he loved what he did and was also very good at delivering it. He made his clients feel like they were his number one priority. This meant that he had a certain cache with a particular clientele able to do just that and he became confident in commanding excellent remuneration fees. The Cartwright women were in a position to pay well, inheriting much of their parents' wealth after their father passed away in his early fifties leaving them well inherited but parentless. Sassy, Clemmie and Ora had supported each other from the age of twenty-two and stayed together ever since in the house where they had grown up. Any romantic suiters soon found out where they were in the pecking order in this family of siblings. They were fiercely loyal and protective of each other.

He pulled on his favourite fitness kit. He wanted to look good for his girls and maybe one in particular. Checking himself out in the mirror he studied his teeth, ran his hand over his hair and took a body building pose. He liked what he saw, smiled a broad Lamont smile, danced down the stairs, moved to sweep up his keys and opened the door.

>>> <<<

'I was taken by Lamont's collection of vinyl you know. I actually found it interesting,' said Sassy.

'I came home and started reading about the art work in sixties music particularly. Wow. You know what it's like when you start browsing and surfing. I was thinking about Balwinder and wandered into film scripts. That was interesting too! I ended up in a scroll hole and couldn't get to sleep.'

Clemmie and Ora cast a knowing look at each other. Sassy always threw herself into pet subjects. 'Apparently, there are so many different approaches to script collecting. He told me some people prefer a final, revised draft as close as possible to the completed film. Others get caught up with earlier drafts. There are even those who get off searching out a variety of drafts of the same film!'

Sassy laughed and flicked her long auburn hair back in a gesture of flippancy. Her sisters copied in unison in an act of togetherness.

'Honestly Sassy let's not get too wrapped up in Andrew's big idea. I know he means well but is it that interesting?' Ora replied. 'Or is it that you want to impress someone with your knowledge? Like a stalking praying mantis preparing to strike at the unsuspecting male.'

'You know I think it might be. I actually find the poor intellectual soul quite attractive. They have genuine interest and enthusiasm for their subjects.' Ignoring the gentle jibes of her sisters she returned to the topic. 'There are scripts that are pristine while others have been highlighted. Sometimes actors highlight their lines or write notes to the dialogue.'

'Oh, please, enough,' said Clemmie. 'Let's talk about the people rather than the thing. It's all rather tedious. Andrew is such a nice fellow but stamps – please. Interesting yes but thrilling no. Let's stick with what we know girls; handbags and perfume. It's what we take satisfaction in and share our pleasure. That's what we were told to do at the gathering.' There was much nodding of approval with varying levels of enthusiasm and the team returned to a shared view as they so often did.

The girls had followed their father's instruction to the letter. Losing the mother they had never known that in some way could have been their fault had a profound effect on the family. It created a bond that always made them stick together. The stress of carrying three babies and delivering them was too much for her undiagnosed heart condition. Their father, in between bouts of exoteric writings, had picked up the reigns of parenthood and through his grief raised the girls well. Alan Cartwright had met the love of his life at university where they were both enjoying their passion for literature and creative writing. She, from a wealthy family and he from, what was known then as, a broken home. They engaged in a passionate romance and enjoyed a joyous early marriage until tragedy struck with the birth of the girls.

He had loved them beyond measure and had thrown his total energies into ensuring their welfare. They in return had adored him. He had managed to publish a series of novels as they grew up and provided for them not least in respect of a private education as day pupils at the local private school. His creation of the winning character Randolph X, the hero protagonist, had taken centre stage in a series of space adventure books including 'Jupiter Moon', 'Mercury Rising' and 'Mars Attack'. This successful series had brought in impressive and enduring royalties and cemented a reputation for outstanding science fiction writing. The tragedy of them then losing their father as well as their mother while still only young adults made their bond ever tighter. Although their financial situation was secure through their property and financial inheritance their confidence to introduce young men into the relationship was difficult given their close bond of protective loyalty to each other.

They had all attended Birmingham University rather than leave home and had lost their father just over a year after graduating. It was in their studies that they realty celebrated their differences across the arts, sciences and technologies. Entering university without a career in mind they chose a course of study that stimulated them and which their father had encouraged. Sassy had chosen design; Clemmie software development and Ora, business marketing. All had left after three years with good honours degrees and had all been successful in taking up posts with companies in their chosen fields. Eighteen months later and too confident in their own abilities to be employed they had set up their own web-based design start-up company with the support of their father. It was a competitive market.

One month later their father was dead from a massive heart attack. This had really made the girls grow up; not that they had needed anymore heart ache. They had inherited enough of a work ethic to dig deep and make the business work, generally agreeing that Sassy took charge, Clemmie was the brains of the operation and Ora would do a lot of the face-to-face business when needed. They found they complemented each other well.

Now eight years later, they were well established, independent and secure but as thirty-one-year-old women they had all discussed and were aware of their choices in entering the reproductive time line, finding the right eligible men, the role of family and more recently fertilisation options.

'That may be so Clemmie,' retorted Ora, 'and I can't say I disagree with you but in about twenty minutes Sassy be fixated on Lamont and swooning over his good looks, offering him sycophantic appreciation and fawning over his vinyl records!' Sassy oozed a strong personal presence. With unusual green eyes, a pale complexion and a wide endearing smile that flowered her mouth like two large petals to show a wonderfully perfect set of white teeth. She was unaware of the impact of her strong physical presence on the others. Ora, not to be overshadowed by her taller sister, pulled on her Sweaty Betty sports bra and pants and began limbering up. 'Have you noticed that our big sister won't let us near the personal training accounts. I'm beginning to wonder about the amount of gratuity being added.'

'I think not my dear. I am interested in his musical taste only out of politeness. Look at you. I think you're the one who wants to impress,' retorted Sassy 'but you haven't got the balls.'

Clemmie hated it when her sisters got catty. It didn't show either of them in a good light.

'Well that's a relief,' retorted Ora lifting the atmosphere. All three sisters broke into a spontaneous giggle.

The sound of a gentle knock on the door thankfully broke their conversation.

'I'll answer that, you two get ready as quickly as possible. I don't want to waste our schedule. You know what Lamont is like.' Ora ran down the stairs to the entrance hall and invited Lamont through into a large ante room prepared for activity with mats, skipping ropes, dumb bells and exercise balls.

'How are you today, Ora?'

'All the better for seeing you Lamont,' said Ora, pouting her lips, pushing back her hair and fluttering her eye lashes flirtatiously which made a strobe effect of her big blue eyes 'and looking forward to our workout. Got anything new for us?'

'Of course. As always. I like to keep you three on your toes,' came the reply.

'I'll need to be on my toes to kiss those lips Lamont,' she said continuing the flirtation.

Lowering her voice to almost a whisper and pushing her head towards his ear Ora breathed,

'Make sure you make me look good against the others. You know the exercises I'm good at and they're not and after all I am your favourite.' She blushed as if she had planned it and was able to redden her face on demand. Lamont smiled and nodded kindly in acknowledgement. It was hard to say no to Ora, which was sometimes difficult because of the three women, he was conscious that he held a stronger affection in her sister Sassy's favour.

'Lamont, so good to see you.'

'A timely interjection,' he thought. 'So good to see you too Clemmie,' he said really meaning it. 'Let's get Sassy in here and we can start.'

'I'm here,' came the voice from the staircase and a beaming, white teeth smile arrived seconds later.

'Right ladies, let's get going. Music on, faces glowing……'

The boom of 'All the Single ladies, all the single ladies' got the session started.

Lamont stretched his more than sufficient body and the sisters loved it, effortlessly copying his rhythmically smooth movements.

5. Financial Fireworks.
5th November 2022. (Before)

Elise Goodrich stood in the bay of her bedroom window watching the world go by. Not that much of the world went by in her quiet Bromsgrove tree lined avenue. A few parked cars belonging to owners looking for quick access into the high street without a parking fee; one or two essential workmen – a perennial these days – not like when she was younger; and a solitary jogger treading out his well-worn route. You could tell the time by him. College Road was an old, broad, quiet and well-established avenue in the town. She was happy with this even when the large houses with large plots started being taken for care homes and dentists. Elise didn't worry. She loved the familiar and there was still plenty of that. Like her people. Plenty who were like here. Values, standards, rules, law and order. That's what sets us apart she mused. That is what makes us great. She contemplated her conversations of the other evening and her enjoyment in meeting collectors of various persuasions. Andrew's stamps, Lamont's vinyl and Maximillian's cars. Best of all, her niece's handbags; not really surprising since it was she who, along with what they had inherited from their mother, had given the girls much of their collection. Elise had been good to the triplets when her sister died. It was a tragic time for all the family and they needed her support but their father had been remarkable in his commitment to his children. She had stood in of course and provided some aspects of motherhood surrogacy to the girls as they grew up but their father had been magnificent in his care for them all. Oh, and Lickey's jewellery; quite exceptional. That was definitely the best of the evening and the conversation the most engaging ... the jewellery. The timepiece now in her hand particularly. Old coins are very interesting she thought, but not as pretty. She had her own collection of course and wore most of it on a daily basis. No real pleasure locking this away or storing in a dusty box. She clipped the encrusted diamond Rolex on her slim wrist and was thankful for how well it took attention away from her ageing hand.

She saw the old red mini clubman draw up on her open driveway and the worried face of Sangita Sangar emerge graciously from the drivers' side. Sangita raised her head and acknowledged her with a faint smile and raised her hand. She used her hand to brush back her ebony hair and quickly wipe her large brown eyes before disappearing beneath the entrance porch. Elise paced slowly across the room and down the curving flight of stairs to the reception and opened the door.

'Sangita, do come in. I'm just about to boil the kettle. Tea or coffee?'

Thanks for inviting me over Elise. Have you anything a little stronger? I'm in need of a sedative.' Sangita, dressed in her delicately ornate silk orange and blue Sari, a strong symbol of her Indian cultural tradition, followed Elise into the kitchen.

'Come through and tell me all about it and let's see if we can work out a recovery strategy or an exit plan at the very least. Try not to worry. Nobody is dead!'

'I'm such a fool Elise. There seemed so much easy gain to be made and I feel I have over stretched. The promotion was so aggressive and the figures so alluring I am afraid I stopped thinking.'

'You're not the first and you won't be the last. That's the hidden master plan I'm afraid. Coin is at the sharp end of capitalism where there is only the quick, the clever and the dead.' For an older lady Elise still knew how to pack her punches. 'I'm afraid the market preys on weaker elements of human nature, greed being one of them; it sucks you carefully in until, like the cobra, it chooses to strike. What have you bought?'

'I traded fifteen thousand pounds into crypto currency on the twenty seventh of March and it's fallen off a cliff since then. I now have less than seven thousand pounds worth of coin as of this morning.'

'Hold your nerve dear. The market is the market,' said the gracefully ageing but wise lady handing over a glass of Darroze Grand Assemblage and settling into her favourite chair.

'As long as you can afford the hit it can be left to recover', Elise went on. 'It's all numbers on a screen until you need to cash it in.'

'But what if it goes down to nothing. I will have lost it all.' A silent tear rolled down Sangita's cheek. 'Do you think I should pull out now?'

'It all depends if the seven thousand pounds you have means more than the eight thousand that you may recover my dear. The whole investment market is a gamble really and it's amplified in on-line crypto currency. There is no such thing as easy money Sangita and the sum you've traded has obviously got you in over your head. What have you traded into?'

'Ethereum.'

'Well not the worst of them. I'd stick it out and see what happens in 2023. As soon as you get some partial recovery to the level of loses you could sustain get out fast. It's not worth the stress or the unhappiness. I say this as friend and not as a financial adviser.'

'Thank you Elise. You are such a good friend to me. I don't know what I'd do without you.'

'We all have our cross to bear Sangita. Thank Christopher in this respect. I got all my financial acumen from him God bless his soul. While you are missing your money I am missing him. You may get your money back but I know in this life he is lost to me forever. I wish he was still with me now.'

'I know my dear. You will not and cannot forget him. He had a big heart, a big love for you and a big fondness for the town. He was such a good member of parliament for us all and taken from us too early.'

'That is true but he would want me to honour him by continuing to support the town he loved. I do this through my work with the Bromsgrove Court Leet; keeping a watching eye on my nieces Sassy, Clemmie and Ora and supporting my friends who are close to me of which you are one.'

Sangita raised her glass in recognition and managed a seasoned smile. She knew she relied on Elise for guidance on so many things and she never let her down. She considered her a true friend; someone that she could count on in good and bad times. It wasn't that Elise always found a solution to the problem and she could be very direct but she, like others in her orbit, always felt better for the conversation with her. There was an inherent kindness in her and she had her trust.

6. The Court Leet.
9th November 2022. (Before)

The members of the Court gathered around the room, some standing, some sitting, most idly chatting; some joking and some deep in conversation. The Autumn Court was yet to be called to order and the mood of the room seemed light and somewhat jovial as the Bailiff prepared himself, silently looking over the agenda.

Elise sat in eager anticipation of today's presentation. After all, it was her protégé who was about to speak. She had introduced him to the Leet twelve months ago after giving him chapter and verse regarding its history. She smiled across the room at me as I encouraged members to take their seats.

The Ancient Court Leet and Court Baron of the manor of Bromsgrove', she had explained to Lamont at length, 'was established by royal charter in 1199. It was granted by King John and had a historical sphere of influence stretching from Chadwick and Lickey Common in the north to Buntsford and Timberhonger in the south and from Dodcote and Woodford in the east to Burcot and Shepley in the west'.

She had gone onto elucidate that 'the word leet, denoted a territorial and a jurisdictional area that became common in England in the **thirteen hundreds;** where a private lord could assume power that had previously been exercised by a sheriff'.

Lamont was hooked as Elise went on.

'He could also make money from the courts through the impositions of fines, a proportion of which was returned to the crown in the form of a levy or tax', she had said adding that in modern times the Court Leet only functioned to uphold tradition and preserve the towns heritage'.

'Yes,' Lamont had said 'but what purpose does it serve today?'

She took a second to take a breath and continued.

'It serves now only to manage common land, give people a voice and organise and attend charitable events and had no legal power of enforcement; but its more than that. This is a piece of English history and we need to preserve it. If we don't know where we've been how do we work out where we're going,' she had said.

Lamont could not deny that social history and his own sense of ceremony had attracted him. He had sat quietly listening to Elise and had grown increasingly inquisitive. She in turn was not ready to finish. It is their responsibility to uphold history and tradition and make it fit the modern world if it is worth it she had said. That is why I wanted to involve Lamont and why she thought it would be a good thing for him. There had been funny moments at the start with Lamont's interjection in the court leet meeting where he had called me, as the reeve the referee and when corrected he asked who'd blown the whistle on him.

He was astute in his knowledge of British history and knew well enough that medieval England was feudal in nature and the Lord of the Manor had certain rights over his serfs and tenants. He also knew that the Lord could hold sway over administrative concerns. He did not know that the Court Leet dealt with issues ranging from nuisances, affray or assault, selling faulty goods, using false weights and measures, to playing unlawful games, keeping disorderly alehouses, disturbing the peace and keeping inmates and vagabonds. 'Maybe we should hand those powers back,' he had ventured.

By the nineteen seventies there were only thirty-three court leets exempted from abolition by the Administration of Justice Act of that year, many still functioning today including Bromsgrove

They both knew people in the group. Maximillian held the title of Reeve, deputy to the Bailiff and as a result was responsible for ensuring decisions of the leet were enacted and summoning the jury when needed. He was proud of the role and took his position seriously. He too also enjoyed the ceremonial aspect of his involvement so in keeping with his self-perceived social status and he was keen to make a contribution. The Court consisted of honorary and hereditary positions such as the Lord of the Manor and internally elected positions such as the Bailiff, the Reeve and the Marshal. Jury of men represented many ancient trades such as 'Bread weigher' and 'Carniter and Fish taster'; and ealdormen one of whom was elected Bailiff for a year.

It was definitely not democratic. Once a member always a member unless you resigned or reached the age of seventy-five.

'Listen Lamont, Andrew Byron is a member and has been since 2009', she had told him.

I like to think that in this small way I helped to cement his decision to offer his services.

As the now elected steward, I called the meeting to order. Maximillian after stirring attention outside by arriving in his cobalt blue 1996 2.4 V6 Royale Sabre two-seater convertible, took his seat between the Bailiff and the Chaplain, the vicar of St Johns Church, who led a prayer for the town. Max with obvious disregard for the solemnity scanned the room during the prayer to take in those present as if examining those worthy of his presence.

I read through the agenda and called upon Lamont Adams to report on highway matters and district enforcement measures. Lamont took his cue graciously. He had been sponsored by Elise, the only female member of the Leet and his name had been promoted in an effort to add diversity to the group which had gained comprehensive, though not unanimous, support. She had fought hard enough to break the male strangle hold that existed on the Leet and continued to be an irritant to those she had privately labelled as 'old duffers'. There had been resignations when Elise joined and there were more when Lamont became a member. He had little prior knowledge of the group but had been interested to learn more. Since his nomination and acceptance by the bailiff he had invested time and energy in liaising with district council officials and thereafter becoming an important jury man.

'Honourable Steward, elected officials and members of the jury, I report today on matters pertaining to the infra-structure of Bromsgrove as it continues to grow and prosper and changes to the transportation routes through and around the town as a result of home expansion. Members will already be familiar with the challenges we are facing in additional development and congestion of traffic along the main arterial routes..........'

Whilst Lamont continued his report Elise looked on, proud of his involvement and positive contributions. Maximillian stared into space vacuously. He had not been so keen on Lamont joining the jury men. There was more than a hint of exclusivity in his reasoning arguing that as an ancient tradition, values were not being upheld by the involvement of 'new Britons'. His argument had been shut down quickly by the Sheriff but his comments had not been hard to interpret as race related. Max had been informally labelled a small minded racist from another era and he had not taken kindly to the jibes. In keeping with his nature he refused to admit to that view while never apologising for his remarks. His enmity towards Lamont had only grown as a result and it did little to foster an open and co-operative Leet. Lamont had only learnt of this through awkward private conversations with Elise and his antipathy towards Max had thereafter grown in return. It was not surprising therefore that regular challenges to each other's opinions became a routine in meetings and had to be carefully managed by either the Lord, the steward or the Bailiff.

As a club with appointees made from within and by invitation only, many of the population of Bromsgrove went about its daily business with little regard or a second glance in the direction of the Leet and if asked many wouldn't have known its function or purpose. They saw the town crier perhaps a couple of times a year and saw some strange men in medieval clothes parading around the town for fun equally rarely. Yet behind this quite sheltered façade there was on going animosity between two of its members.

The meeting concluded with questions and answers directed at Lamont which Elise noted he handled with confidence and ease. What are officers doing about the much-needed proposed by-pass? How can traffic be re-routed through the town? Is there money for expanding dual carriageways around the centre? What success has there been with government grants?

Do officers of the authority realise the impact of air pollution on residents? Can he assure the Leet that everything is being done that can be done to hold developers to account in their plans and to limit house building where social infra- structure is inadequate? Will change bring more jobs and consequently more people into the town leading to added problems?

Maximillian nodded his head. Not in agreement but more to do with dropping off to sleep. 'Morons,' he thought as he closed his eyes. 'Dinosaurs and skeletons.' His impatience had got the better of him again but he smiled ruefully; at least it was Lamont facing the questions.

7. Running Up That Hill.
13th November 2022. (Before)

Tardebigge Flight is a set of locks on the approximately thirty-mile-long Worcester to Birmingham canal. The Flight consists of thirty locks, many in quick succession and is the longest set of locks in Great Britain. It stretches a distance of two and a quarter-miles in which the canal is raised sixty-six metres on its journey to Birmingham. In its time it has transported porcelain pots and Cadbury's chocolate between the two cities.

Lamont had joined the tow path at the site of the Navigation Inn and was running up towards Tardebigge reservoir. It was a cold November day and he was dressed for the elements with a white synthetic base layer and a blue and grey lightweight waterproof running jacket with black running tights . He adjusted his grey running gloves and the grey merino beanie hat while he ran. It was probably more of a habit rather than a necessity. He had learnt from experience that winter running could quickly become a negative experience for the poorly prepared. He looked at his watch and was pleased with his time so far. He felt good as he ran up and past the next watering hole at the Queens Head that sat seductively on the other bank. He looked left towards it and was reminded of the meeting with Andrew and Max three weeks earlier. He smiled at Andrew's persistence to get a collectors society up and running.' Acorns to oak trees,' he thought. It was only then that he realised why Andrew had chosen the Queens Head for that initial meeting; it was a metaphor that acutely referenced his stamp collecting. 'Why didn't I see that before,' he wondered, allowing himself a little laugh between breaths.

He was enjoying the eight-mile course; he used it regularly, rain and shine, trying to fit the long jog in once a week as he was aware of his propensity to bulk up easily. The run helped keep him lean while most of his work kept him supple and strong. It also provided some quiet time to think and plan – he was becoming increasingly successful and wanted to keep it that way by preparing for the next step. He loved his work for the activity it provided. He was not a sitter and felt mentally better for the exercise and for the healthy living he was able to nurture.

He remembered he still had a distance to go and understanding his capacity he dropped his pace. He ran on navigating what was, in keeping with the season, a wet and treacherous route in parts and travelled up the course under five bridges before levelling out by the high bank of the reservoir. His trainers and lower legs were splattered with the wet and muddy water he was all too familiar with.

It began to rain lightly and he could feel the gentle patter as the drops hit is face. He looked up to the top of the reservoir bank and immediately recognised Bart Bramble deep in discussion with what looked like and what he considered to be a rather unsavoury character. The two were involved in an exchange and Lamont recognised it for what it was straight away. He had seen his fair share of these exchanges growing up. 'Well, well,' he thought. 'I would never have guessed.' Bart was too focused to notice the well clad athlete who ran on the spot, turned and jogged back the way he came He wondered what drugs Bart was using. It must be recreational and probably explained Bart's unworried nature. He laughed out aloud in surprise as he left the canal path onto Upper Gambolds Lane heading towards Aston Fields. Why was he surprised?

Politicians seemed to be the worst – moralising whilst having to admit a misspent youth later.

He passed the Tennis and Hockey club on his left – Ora was probably there training but this was no time to stop. His mind wandered onto her sister Sassy Cartwright; his efforts to establish a stronger relationship with her was paying off and the intervention he had made with Max had been appreciated. Little did she know how he had achieved that desired aim. Sassy, Max, Sangita and now Bart; all with a Bromsgrove story waiting to be told. He hadn't thought the town was so interesting when he had moved there for a more relaxed pace and the chance to embrace its quiet serenity. 'Not so serene anymore,' he quipped to himself. He slowed down as he turned into Churchfields and took the last few steps to home at a walking pace. He removed his trainers and jacket before opening the door, felt for the key in the right pocket and opened the door. He had a plan to shower and then watch the Sao Paolo Grand Prix and then go over the Balwinder's place for a drink. Max would be there but he would not let that spoil his fun.

8. The Dream.
10th November 2022. (Before).

It was eleven thirty in the morning. I know because I had taken an early lunch break and just checked my watch when suddenly it happened out of nowhere. A swishing near silent viciousness; there was no curdling scream nor a splash of blood. Clemmie first melting and writhing on the ground forming quickly into an icy stillness. A guttural drawl and then silence. Not even running footsteps. I looked down and then instinctively around and where there had been a black cloud and a rushing steam of heat there was nothing. I returned my gaze to the floor and Clemmie, her delicate lips oozing a pool of dark crimson blood that soaked away into the pavement cracks. Whatever I did or thought I would do was too late for her. I gathered her in my arms and held her close. 'Clemmie wake up, wake up' but I knew she wouldn't. I snatched my phone from the chest pocket of my jacket and pumped the numbers 999 into it.

'What service do you require.'

'Ambulance. St Johns Cemetery, Bromsgrove.... quickly. There's no pulse and I think she may be already dead.'

I had 'phoned Sassy and Ora immediately as a small crowd of faceless onlookers gathered, some helpful some not. They arrived at the same time as the paramedics. Clemmie was pronounced dead at the scene. The sisters were understandably inconsolable. I was still in shock. There were people about – it was a cemetery after all and a common walkway to and from town – who saw nothing.

I had contacted work who thankfully were concerned and worried about me – who wouldn't? I would have been useless anyway my thoughts were all over. Death had only fleetingly touched me though the passing of ageing relatives; not friends and never in suspicious circumstances.

>>> <<<

'And what happened next Andrew?' said Clemmie, holding on to every moment of the dream I had just recounted to her.

'I woke up in a bed damp with sweat, breathing heavily and perspiration on my forehead. It was all too real Clemmie. I really thought I'd lost you.'

'Oh, you dear thing Andrew,' she said leaning in and kissing my cheek affectionately. 'I do hate those all too real dreams. They do, however, expose us to our deepest thoughts. I rather like the idea that you don't want to lose me. My guess is it's more to do with Max than me though.' This coming from a woman who had experienced significant loss in her life a number of times brought a gulp to my throat. It was true though that Max had been occupying my thoughts.

'I mean it Clemmie. I do hold loving thoughts for you and you are important in my life.' She squeezed my sleeve without saying anything further and we walked on through the High Street arm in arm. 'Perhaps I should save up more anxiety dreams to tell you if this is what we get to,' I thought. We stopped outside the bank.

'I just need to pop in here for a moment Andrew, don't go anywhere.'

'Not likely,' I thought. 'Here is where I want to be.'

I gazed up and down the High Street and my eyes fell upon the statue of A.E Houseman staring down at me inquisitively. I had passed this proud pose hundreds of times but never found the time to read the inscription. Born and raised in and around Bromsgrove he had lived in a small hamlet of the town called Fockbury for much of his life. It was and still is a short walk from the centre of Bromsgrove leaving town via Churchfields, up Fockbury Mill Lane and across the motorway towards Dodford.

I bent to read the inscription on the plinth taken from his most famous work, 'A Shropshire Lad':

From far, from eve and morning
And yon twelve winded sky
The stuff of life to knit me
Blew hither; here am I

My particular leaf had not blown far but life had certainly knit me. Should I blow my own course more fervently or see where the wind takes me, I thought. I was scared that I may blow too strong but what are dreams for?

Clemmie emerged from the bank.

'Right Andrew. Where shall we go now?'

'Heaven or hell,' I thought and took her by her shoulders and kissed her passionately on the lips. She did not pull away. I remember that more than anything. The world passed by whilst we stood still in those moments.

Afterwards we walked silently on to Church Lane and past St Johns walk onto Worcester Road. The next thing I knew we were in the Stoney Hill area of town. We strolled past Balwinder Singh's house. As we paced along the pavement bordered by the expansive grounds of the town's private school I felt a very private smile slipping over my face. I glanced down at Clemmie. She was smiling too but not just from her mouth. Her whole face was radiating warmth and love.

I had not felt like this for years – not since becoming a widower – and I daresay I will never feel like it again. I was elated that she was watching me. It wasn't the lady walking her dog or the two children chatting, appearing as if they were still slowly returning home from school. There was nothing out of the ordinary about the old man carrying his shopping bag. He looked vaguely familiar but it was after all a small town; maybe it was the moment but I felt there were eyes on us, all secretly sharing our moment. We began to descend along the familiarly named 'Pig Alley', which was in fact a pleasant walkway leading to the local high school and erstwhile school children's smokers hide. The walk had helped me to calm myself and to regulate both my breathing and my mind. We decided it was time to go home to my small terrace property that lay on a small recess off the Worcester Road called Peters Finger.

The light was starting to fade and the dim light of the streetlamps started to shimmer in the cold November air as we turned right onto Charford Road. Five minutes later we were in the comfort of my home holding a warm drink and listening to the Bodyguard soundtrack – a vinyl album that Lamont had bought me and a sentiment that was not wasted on me now. We fell asleep together in my armchair and into sweet oblivion.

9. A Game of Consequence.
12th November 2022. (Before)

I sat at my desk gazing at my work screen. 'What have I done? What was I thinking? On the High Street in full view of the town. The town where I grew up, where I am deeply invested, where I am well known and recognisable. Who am I to threaten her status, her confidence her relationships? Where was my head? Without doubt I love and care for Clemmie but was I overstepping in the wrong place and the wrong time. What train of events have I set in motion…….?'

Meanwhile, Clemmie sat at her dresser looking in the mirror. She smiled to herself and saw her cheeks flush in the mirror. 'Wow I wasn't expecting that,' she thought aloud. She knew the attention given to her over time was genuine and sincere. She knew the affection for her had always been real but this was a whole new level and she liked it. Her only real concern was how her sisters would react. Was it a breach of faith? A breaking of the bond between them? A treachery and deception? Did Andrew think that too and knew how I felt but had denied it. She had certainly flirted but without expectation. After all there was nine years between them and was he more of a platonic love? Obviously he didn't think so. Did she like him because he was safe? Did he offer her security and solidity but she had never anticipated passion......

At the same time, I paced around the office unable to concentrate. The church steeple frowned down upon me seemingly bending through the window and raindrops rolled down the glass like tears, before the sun suddenly brought a smiling rainbow that captured the town sky line. This is ridiculous I thought; I, a widower and nine years her senior. Snap out of it. My feelings are honourable and true. I have nothing to regret. What have you to offer her? my contentious self countered. I am hardly a modern-day lothario which could be good but what ambition can I show her? I have grown up in Bromsgrove, went to an excellent school, left with good qualifications but whilst others left for universities and ventures further afield my life adventure stayed in the town in a safe job and limited prospects. Is that all I offer.......?

I do like him a lot. Do I love him? He is a lot older than me and a widower to boot. Clemmie mused. She had not experienced a lot of this type of attention even from men of her own age. Not because she was not attractive. She was a natural in many ways. Not one to dress up too often but rather dress down, she preferred jeans and sweat tops to anything else. She knew how to dress to impress and looked stunning when she did. She knew that but her loyalty to her sisters and her fear of loss had frozen a part of her life. The girls would know. They always did. All three had telepathic understanding of each other.......

'Nonsense, all nonsense. I know how I feel and I will not be dissuaded. Love conquers all. This is the girl for me.' I logged out of my computer, and leaving my desk walked out of the door sensing the eyes of the office on me. Had I said that too loudly? I didn't stop to find out.......

Clemmie felt a wave of emotion pass through her. She had reflected on all the things that she and Andrew had shared and experienced. It was a slow burn she had to admit but she couldn't deny her feelings. This was a defining moment and she knew it.......

10. The Aftermath.
14th November 2022. (After)

The town was in shock. Max had many circles of friends and acquaintances. His parents, like a world full of parents before and after them, were besides themselves never expecting to outlive their own son. In their most sanguine moments they recognised that his recklessness was always a cause for concern and at some point his risk taking might catch up with him. At other times they were inconsolable. I sat with them a lot over the coming weeks as they tried to come to terms with what had happened. All I could do was listen and recount tales that sometimes made them laugh or at least smile through the tears. I had taken them to identify the body; a task that was hard on all of us. It brought back unhappy memories for me, having had to complete a similar ritual years earlier for my then wife Madelaine, who I had tragically lost after a short illness whilst in her twenties. Granted it was not to identify her but it was all the more painful for it. It did make me question why this had happened to two people so close to me but one can't dwell too long on these thoughts. I had long held the view that there are plenty of people in the world worse off than I. Max's stoical parents for example who would lean on me for months afterwards and who I was only too happy to help.

Then there was his rugby club. He had a presence there on and off the pitch. His position as a blindside flanker had given him a role of shutting down the opposition scrum half. A position he loved. He became the 'blonde bomber' who relished the clear and simple challenge. He was totally at home in the clubhouse after matches recanting tales, laughing at his exploits and usually mocking and ridiculing others performances. These were usually taken in good spirits along with the ale consumed. One would have thought that he was an international player rather than the second team regular that he was. There would be a hole in that clubhouse for some time.

Next his automobile fraternity. Not really a petrol head club but a fan of the car itself, its history and its design features. There was a hastily arranged drive past his house from his fellow car enthusiasts. He actually owned four cars. Two sat on the roadside close to his home and the other two were garaged at his parent's home. There was a lot to be organised and his parents had asked me to help. Of course the Morgan had been impounded by the police but that left me to look after the future of the blue Royale Sabre as well as a 1967 twin exhaust MG midget convertible in flame red and a 2010 4.7 V8 Maserati Granturismo in white. The Maserati was his most valued possession but he loved the 1987 3.5 Morgan the best and had spent most of the time on the road in it. Fitting then, that he had spent his final moments behind it's wheel. It was a modest collection of cars to many with a value of approximately sixty thousand pounds worth of investment and they had all been his pride and joy. I shed a silent tear as I remembered his loving enthusiasm for all of them. There would be willing buyers but I wondered if there was a way I could keep them together in memory of him? I determined I would at least try for his sake. He would have liked that.

I remembered his smile. That would be a lasting memory. He could melt an iceberg with that smile. Even Max, God bless his soul, whose outrageousness gave vent to humour when he failed to suffer fools, often brought his own peculiar bon vivant to the party. I remembered his hilarious jousting with Sangita over modern art. He had spoken what others had feigned to think. I pictured the scene.

'Nothing more than the Kings clothes. No talent, no skill and no sense. The modern art movement has successfully brainwashed an entire generation beguiling it with their freedom of expression art bollocks.'

Sangita had taken it in good humour but had been determined to provide a counter so as not to be outdone. This was her world and she wanted to defend it.

'Art provokes and questions. It evokes emotions. You are a living exemplification to the success of Art to do these things. Art can be liked disliked but seldom ignored. It still remains Art, Max.'

'You see what I mean. Art bollocks all over again. You can't win an argument against artists they'll just want to churn out the same old tripe.'

'True …and false,' said Sangita smiling.

'There you are. I rest my case,' said Max, appearing exasperated and exhausted at the same time but in reality they had both enjoyed the good-humoured exchange.

The next meeting of the Court Leet had held a minutes silence and a short speech from the Baron in his honour. From the corner of my eye I had glanced over towards Lamont and Elise, their heads bowed in respectful observation. I resolved in that moment to honour Max in a similar vein at the next gathering of collectors. He would have liked that.

11. An Inspector Calls.
29th December 2022. (After)

The constabulary were quick off the mark and two days later I was sitting in Hindlip police station after receiving a call inviting me to an informal discussion that 'may help with our enquiries'. I had resisted a home visit and noted a preference to a discussion at the station as Peter's Finger was a small approach with only a few houses . I was uncomfortable about having a police car outside my house that may have added fuel to the already circulating story. Social media was already concocting its own theories but I fully accepted that my account of the hours before death would be useful to the investigation.

'Thank you for coming in this morning Mr Byron,' Detective Inspector Raymond Chandler said, casting a wave of his hand as an invitation to sit down. I picked up a well-spoken yet soft rolling accent, perhaps Gloucestershire/Somerset border country. I accepted the gesture and sat down on the functional wooden chair he had suggested. He sat opposite me in a more formal manner than I thought necessary. I was a little disappointed in the room as I had half expected to see all the photos of the suspects on the wall with string linking their evidential movements. I had imagined the victim having a central position on the wall too. I had watched enough crime films over the years to make that assumption. Instead the walls were empty bar a calendar with some illegible scribblings and some posters telling me that crime doesn't pay and dial nine-nine-nine only in an emergency. I guessed the coffee machine in the corner of the room played a significant role in the daily life of an investigative policeman.

He continued. 'Let me tell you I am not a convention-al investigator Mr Byron. I am going to tell you things that I already know so that you can tell me what you already know more easily. The sharing of information elucidates and oils the works leading to full expression, yet at times can lead me into choppy waters if confidence is broken. Do I make myself clear?'

I didn't feel empowered enough to say no so I just nodded my head.

'Good. Whilst I await the full report from the Coroner's Office I am tasked to make enquiries to establish the events surrounding the death of Mr Maximillian

Charles and whether there was any evident intent that could form a possible criminal investigation. I have invited you here to help in the investigation; you are not under caution and you may leave at any time.'

I was relieved to hear it. The inspector had piercing blue eyes that I felt were already burning a route through to my soul.

'Although there initially appeared to be no unusual suspicions surrounding Mr Charles's death, there were routine elements of the circumstances that required post mortem. As I have said, the pathologist report is as yet to be completed but he has indicated the discovery of traces of cocaine during autopsy at a concentration level of one point one two milligrams per litre that was laced with fentanyl. 'I understand you may still be in shock but it is important that we understand the cause of death and the circumstances that surrounded it. As you were one of the last people to see him alive you and your friends are in an important position to help me piece together his last few hours.'

Stopping only briefly to draw breath he continued.

'Further medical examination indicates that Mr Charles appears to also have sustained injuries that contributed to his death. He had a ruptured spleen and a broken right hip as a result of a collision with a tree that smashed the driver side of the car.' Her paused for thought and air. He took a deep breath. 'Unusually though he was also a victim of a rare aneurism of the splenic artery. The other interesting finding relates to blunt force trauma to the frontal cranium, suggestive of high-speed contact of the head with the steering wheel but the nature of the injuries sustained are problematic and inconsistent with the accident.'

I was taken aback by all of this. I had assumed that the car crash had killed him.

'This is significant; the rupture to the artery could have been the cause of the accident and the injuries sustained in the accident were the most likely cause of death or the other way round. A link between the two findings is very likely.'

He paused sitting back, resting his elbows on the arms of his chair and linking his fingers across his torso.

'So these early significant findings lead to further necessary investigation into this case. I have discovered so far through expert testimony and a little reading around the subject that although rare, women are four times more likely to suffer a splenic artery aneurysm than men. Either way these rarely rupture. One in ten patients die from internal bleeding but it is most unusual for a sudden death to occur as in the vast majority of cases. There are typically symptoms and consequent diagnosis leading to a better prognosis for many that don't fit the narrative in this case.' DI Raymond Chandler retained a solemnity as he spoke that I guessed came with the job. He certainly carried an impressive gravitas.

'Oh' I replied not knowing what else to say. I gathered myself together. 'You surprise me inspector,' I said. 'I have never known Max to take any form of drugs; he didn't even smoke cigarettes as far as I was aware.'

Max's death was so sudden and upsetting to recall and I was still having trouble assimilating everything and now came this surprise. For all his failings I had found him an entertaining and interesting character. Yes, he could be a social agitator and provocateur but he was intelligent and often insightful. Although his senior I had known him since my school days. We had both been day boys at the towns independent school which in itself had been a unifying bond. As a senior student and close neighbour I had taken him under my wing; initially walking him to school and then watching him grow to be the over-confident and then the oft annoying but alluring individual he became. By the age of fifteen he was already my physical superior but even then he always took my counsel. He aware I think that I had his true interests at heart from years of support. Max left school with a mediocre set of formal qualifications and was able to get by with what he was given both genetically and financially, eventually gaining a position with a prominent estate agent. First as an 'office hand' and eventually a selling agent, a position well suited to him and he had thrived in presenting and promoting homes to potential buyers earning commission as he went. On reflection I think that is why the friendship had continued. He, like me, had seen many of our contemporaries fly the nest to further education and career opportunities whilst we had both remained in the town of our birth. Nevertheless, he had left a gap in my life and I felt poorer for his passing.

He had lived in his family home up until he was twenty-one when he was gifted his Chaddesley Corbett mews home by his parents who probably thought it was the only way to actually get rid of the daily trauma of living with him. He was a classic 'failure to launch' male stereotype and yet he was misunderstood in some ways. He cared deeply for the town and for his friends. He could be kind and generous and would donate his time and his money to things that he thought worthy. That is not to say he did not have some failings as his brain lacked a filter and he did not recognise some accepted social conventions nor 'suffered fools gladly'. This was an irony in itself as many people would remark he was one himself. I had learnt over time that Max required a firm hand on occasions otherwise he would come over as controlling and opinionated. His views could be narrow and staunch and they needed to be challenged, which could be tiring, but that I had accepted was part of our friendship. Over the years he came to realise that my view was not a criticism of him but merely a different perspective by someone he trusted. I had no doubt that had he been assessed at a younger age or even as an adult he would have been found to be somewhere on the autistic spectrum.

My mind had drifted and I returned to the present.

'I understand,' said Detective Inspector Chandler, 'that all association with death including sudden death, is a sad and sobering experience. For our part, it is the sudden nature and the circumstances that remains unexplained. It is on that basis that I cannot at present close this case. Was Mr Charles a substance abuser? If so, where and when did he obtain cocaine?

Where, why and when did he ingest them? How did he suffer blunt force trauma in the accident? Why was Mr Charles seemingly well and apparently healthy, according to all reports to date, up until the time of his death? What was his true mood? What were you and he talking about and who did he mention? Was he depressed? Did he take his own life? There are so many questions that need to be answered and I am hoping that you and others are able you add something that may give us insights that help us get deeper into this case?'

I remained in silent thought for what seemed like an age but felt honour bound to respond based upon what I had just heard. 'Yes, inspector I think I may be able to give you some additional evidence that may or may not help.' I shifted in my chair trying to get into a more comfortable position both on the outside and the inside for what I was about to say.

12. So far so good.
3rd January 2023. (After)

By the end of the evening of the second of January two thousand and twenty-three DI Raymond Chandler had completed his preliminary discussions. He had personally interviewed fifteen people and organised the constabulary to conduct house to house enquiries in both Chaddesley Corbett and around the streets and homes of the erstwhile supposed friends of Maximillian Charles. He was very aware that all responses to enquiries at this stage were voluntarily made and he was careful not to antagonise or threaten any of his respondents. The following morning he studied his infamous notebook at his station desk. He also had an up-to-date pathology report that had confirmed all preliminary thoughts and so had begun the mental rehearsal of all that he had found out, been told or had gleaned. So far he had established that Andrew Byron was with Max Charles on the eve of the accident, together with Balwinder Singh and Bartholomew Bramble. All three had confirmed their attendance until quarter to eleven when they went their separate ways, apart from Mr Bramble who was offered a lift home by Mr Charles. All three confirmed that Max appeared in good spirits, his mood was good and he showed no signs of depression or overtly negative thoughts. Mr Bramble had stated that he was dropped off by eleven 'o clock at the latest and waved Max goodbye. Bramble thought that Max seemed in a hurry. There were no witnesses who could corroborate this story. Andrew Byron walked home and was in the house by eleven 'o clock. An attentive neighbour saw him approach the house. Mr Singh tidied away the cups and glasses, locked the doors and went to bed. A neighbour here heard the revving of Mr Charles's car on departure and looked out of the window. He saw Balwinder Singh re-enter the house when they had left. This suggested to him that at this stage Andrew Byron and Balwinder Singh were not high on any direct list of direct suspects.

Sangita Sangar had spent the evening with her husband who retired to bed at ten o clock. He had a painful hip and Sangita had encouraged him to taken some tablets to help him sleep. She said she joined him at just before midnight after studying her art work; a fact that her husband hazily recalled as she got into bed.

He had extensive notes on his meeting with Sassy, Clemmie and Ora Cartwright. He was exhausted by the meeting and it had taken a while to decipher their stream of consciousness. The bottom line was they were all working at home on company business until late and had email and social media correspondence to back their story. They were each other's alibi and their time line in respect of company correspondence mean that their direct involvement could all but be ruled out.

Lamont Adams had an early evening dinner date with someone he had met, name withheld or 'rather not say at this stage', from five to eight o' clock. He then visited his parent in Birmingham. He had shared a coffee there and watched TV with them until ten fifteen after which he had driven back to his Churchfields home, arriving at approximately ten-forty-five. DI Chandler had checked out the address and pulled in a favour for a colleague in Moseley who visited the parental home and checked out his attendance. The story was corroborated. Neighbours close to his Churchfields home reported hearing music being played after eleven. His story appeared to stack up.

The Inspector had enjoyed his meeting with Elise Goodrich. 'What a lovely lady,' he had written in large letters. Very bright and well informed she was able to openly share the relationships in this group. Her nieces, her friends, the Collector Club, the Court Leet and other interests and acquaintances. He wrote profusely in that meeting. Ms Goodrich was at home asleep by eleven. She had watched television, finishing with the national news; 'I don't know why Inspector; it's a habit. It always depresses me, so I stop listening before I climb the stairs to bed. I think I must find it soporific.' DI Chandler would not be starting his deeper investigation there.

Lucy Farrier was interesting. She had appeared anxious and nervous but had answered questions thoughtfully and deliberately. He detected a caginess that he had not experienced in other interviews. Her alibi had been Bartholomew Bramble who she received a rather late 'phone call after he returned home that evening. They had been involved in an on-off relationship but they were still friends. 'A 'phone call doesn't prove she was at home though,' he had thought.

The body of Max Charles lay in the morgue as the silent witness. It had already revealed some clues. So far, evidence of narcotic injection, either self-inflicted or by a third party, unusual injuries some in keeping with crash injuries some not, atypical aortic haemorrhage.

He stared into his image visible through the screen save on his computer. 'Well Mr Chandler you have made a fair start. So far so good. Now it's time to bring in the cavalry.'

The cavalry turned out to be a squad rather than a regiment but it was back up none the less.

⪼ ⪻

Anthony Black and Simone Jackson were members of the Investigation Support Team and had been working for the West Midlands force for five and two years respectively. They had a multi-functional role and had worked for DI Chandler before. He considered him a good boss and they liked how he worked. They knew how he functioned, allowing him to think the bigger picture whilst they tied up loose ends and dotted the i's and crossing the t's. He in turn knew that they knew. That is why he liked working with them. The circle was complete. The Inspector lead the meeting.

'So this is where we are. A seemingly tragically fatal but uncomplicated car crash in a convertible Morgan Plus Eight late at night. Likely time around midnight. Roof up windows up. Hypothesis: – victim travelling at speed probably in excess of sixty miles per hour along a winding road. He suddenly brakes and veers to the left probably to avoid something in the road in front of him; possibly a deer, rabbit or badger. Could have been a vehicle coming in the opposite direction but no evidence to point to this. Anyway, he veers at speed, the front near side tyre mounts the curb, the car spins sending it down a small embankment and the driver's door hits the trunk of a large mature English Oak tree. That would seem to have been extremely unlucky. Despite wearing a safety belt he sustains serious injuries, a ruptured spleen, a broken right hip and three broken ribs. He is probably already unconscious at this point, knocked out by the impact to his right temple to the right driver's window. Shattered glass embeds in his right ear and scalp; the right side of his face is badly damaged. No air bag protection on this model of car makes this a very dangerous high velocity impact. The vehicle is slightly hidden by overgrowth and the embankment but it was visible from the road if you were looking out for it. Another five metres either way and the car would probably have ended up in the overgrowth. No one could have planned an accident of this nature so precisely and crash investigator inspection showed no signs of criminal interference. The brakes were functioning and the accelerator free to function so we start from the standpoint of the crash as an accident.'

DI Chandler moved to lift up the crash dummy he has had sent from the central store. He places it on a chair aptly situated next to a structural pillar in the room.

'If the spin takes the car across the curb, down an embankment and into a tree, Max Charles' movements would have been out of his control and he would have been forcibly shaken about. Most of this would have been lateral and as he hit the tree the velocity at impact would force further movement again from side to side.'

He demonstrated the movement by guiding the crash dummy from side to side against the pillar.

'Damage to the temporal skull and subsequent brain damage clearly evident. Why then are there head injuries to the frontal lobe consistent with smashing his head against the steering wheel?'

Anthony Black and Simone Jackson dropped their heads to make notes.

Di Chandler continued.

'So, an appalling accident probably caused through reckless driving and a lack of road awareness. Some alcohol in the blood but below the legal limit that preliminary investigations reveal consistent with his movements prior to the accident. Anyway, critical injuries sustained as I have already said; brain damage, ruptured spleen and broken hip, possibly saveable with quick access from the emergency services. Then, post mortem discovery of inconsistent injuries and needle injection into the left carotid artery administered roughly resulting in bruising before death. Head injuries again inconsistent with a car crash. Drugs present in the body – cocaine and fentanyl. Dangerous to say the least. A fatal dose that was almost certainly administered after the crash. I also hypothesise therefore that there is a very high probability of third-party involvement here and a possible murder charge if we follow the follow the clues and can find a culprit.'

A customary break whilst he gathered his thoughts.

'Whilst we cannot rule out accidental death murder is possible, ladies and gentlemen; opportunistically committed but by whom and for what purpose? We can surmise with some degree of certainly that this is not a random act and therefore was planned but not necessarily for that specific night. Very limited evidence of another person present at the scene although some outline shapes in the mud that could be footprints on the near side of the vehicle possibly size five to seven but no shoe tread identifiable. They could have been there already and the shapes are badly disfigured by branches, leaves and possibly spoilt by the accident itself.'

DI Chandler paused for a further breath and thought. He could feel the blood pumping through his temple and small beads of sweat by his nose on the slope of his cheeks. The case was beginning to drive adrenalin through him as he spoke. He was enjoying the start of the jigsaw but wanted to move off the edges quickly.

'The evidence concerning Max Charles' overall character is mixed,' he continued. 'He has some advocates mostly male, who say he was generally a good egg but who upset people easily – mostly women. His views on equality were apparently outdated and open to testing on a number of fronts. These views, if acted upon, were possibly bordering on criminal. He was small town parochial in his views and seemed slow to get the contemporary picture. A lover of tradition and old-fashioned values. That's not a crime but could upset someone more worldly. As a motive for murder? Still weak. We need a lot more on any one person and at the moment. I have some lightweight suspicions about a number of people but we haven't a strong suspect. This I think is the field,' he said pointing at the names on the board. He turned to address both of his attentive assistants directly.

'So go to the morgue; see what else you can glean from the pathologist. I'm interested in the facial injuries. What's the hypothesis behind them? Get the name of the Constable on the Court Leet; from what I understand from Elise Goodrich about that organisation there is always one and talk to them about their view of the relationship between Max, Andrew Byron, Lamont Adams and Elise Goodrich.' He stared at the names on the board once again.

'I need more on motive and there will and has to be more. Charles was a difficult man. But that's not a justification for murder. See what more you can dig up on Andrew Byron. I thought he was an over willing witness from day one and although I'm of the opinion now that he is a helpful and cooperative soul, I don't want to get over confident in this. The stamp thing worries me but it may be a red herring. Totally unconnected? I'm sure I haven't got the measure of the killer or killers yet and any number of people could just be playing with me. That would lead to why? More likely there a link somewhere.' A short pause and a scratching of the head disturbing the set of his magnificent mane. 'That thread is for later and I'll unpick it in time.'

A rustling of chairs and a shuffling of feet.

'These stamps have got to be connected boss,' said Anthony Black, suddenly conscious of a lose button on his shirt around his ample torso. Realising that he was pursuing an avenue that the Inspector certainly wanted to close off as soon as possible he mumbled, 'Find the sender find the culprit.' Allowing the phrase to fade as he spoke.

'Possibly Tony. We need a break on that front. Keep probing and it will come. Meanwhile I have a bad taste in my mouth that I can't wash away concerning Lickey Farrier. Something doesn't sit right with her story. Dig up all you can on Bart Bramble. He's a prickly customer and see if that bears fruit'.

A timely pun to lighten the room and groans of appreciation came from the Inspectors captive audience and he reminded them of more names whilst he had their attention.

'Lamont Adams and Sassy Cartwright. Something going on there and is it anything that may have a bearing on this case?'

'This could be a nest of vipers sir,' interjected Simone. 'There is so much niceness going around on the surface but what lies beneath could be very different. Should we be looking at seemingly upright folk like Elise Goodrich and Sangita Kumar, apparently great friends to each other but also to the victim? Two apparently outstanding citizens with outstanding credentials but are they vermin or unknowingly in the company of a rat?'

The Inspector gazed fixedly at the small tattoo of a snake on the inside of Simone's wrist to the point that she became self-conscious and feigned to pick up her pen to avoid further scrutiny. The Inspector became aware of his stare and snapped out of his fixed gaze.

'Yes, we know vipers and vermin exist but who and how many?' he queried aloud.

'You are right Simone,' in an attempt to cover the embarrassment of his stare. 'As George Orwell once said, *'all the animals are equals but some are more equal than others'*. No one can be ruled out but at the moment there are two threads of this investigation that I would like you to pull together with me. On the wall in front of you; friends and family of the deceased. My working assumption is just like in many cases, that Max died at the hands of someone he knew. This was not a random pub fight manslaughter. It was planned and executed because of a motive, probably by someone he knew. I have sent you both all of my initial notes from the interviews that I have already conducted. I want you to read them and read them again. Read between the lines, what was said and what wasn't said and why wasn't it said. We'll talk in two days' time and you will give me some more leads to follow from those interviews and discussions.'

The two analysts smiled at each other at the bar of expectation he had set.

'I would also like your summary of door-to-door enquiries. Remember that the bulk of police work often comes from worn shoe leather and what we find there. I would like to find out not only the movements of Max Charles in his village before his demise but also more about the movements of others around his property in the days and hours before his death. The voices of neighbours could be important. It is a small village and my second assumption is that people know a lot of what goes on in these places. Very often more than they want to share.'

He paused again.

'I think that's enough to be going on with. I don't need to remind you of the voluntary nature of any help that can be given. That's still where we are. Be sensitive and set people at ease. That's why

I chose you two – because you're good at it. Let's get going.'

There was another shared ironic smile at his fleeting praise and a nodding of consensus between the pair as they moved their chairs to stand to go about their tasks. They vacated the room in silence leaving DI Chandler to muse over all that he had shared.

Two days later the three sat together once again. 'We have our first piece of luck albeit an expensive one', said Di Chandler. 'We have a hair in the car that does not belong to the victim. Long, probably female, although we cannot not automatically assume as yet. I have pressured our bosses that we need a break and I have agreement that we can test it for DNA although the procedure is costly I think it is worth it. This could be a small break through. What else have we got?'

The two investigative assistants looked at each other and silently agreed that Simone would speak first.

'I went to see Sangita Sangar. In a nutshell and as we already know, she holds Elise Goodrich in very high esteem almost to the point of idolatry. She sees her as a leader in the town and a wise old sage. I wouldn't be surprised if she would follow her off a cliff edge. She spoke of her personal support for her, her commitment to the welfare of her friends and the town. She was very insistent about Elise's honesty and integrity even before I'd asked her about those things. I don't think we can count on Sangita for any disclosures concerning Elise. Having said that, we don't have any strong suspicions around her involvement up to now. When I asked about their relationship with Max she just said he was a slightly flawed yet charismatic character who had a certain appeal. He was a well-known 'marmite personality' in the town. She had heard bad things but she herself had never been on the receiving end of any 'disdainful unpleasantness' as she put it. She had seen others upset by his behaviour and cited Lickey Farrier as a recipient.'

'Quite so Simone. This confirms other reports. Anything else?'

'Ms Goodrich. Just to confirm she has all the appearance of a lovely lady. Long standing high status. Kind, gentle, engaging; one would imagine she would not carry the necessary physicality to take on Max Charles in a fair foot race but that's not a defence. She talked fondly of the victim and although she didn't agree with all his social politics she thought him, in her words and I quote ''a caring soul inside that was shrouded by a tough sometimes irresponsible and un-predictable exterior''.'

They had nothing to add on the stamps save that of confirming that as far as they knew Andrew Byron was the only one with a love for philately.

They went on to discuss the finding at the morgue, the stamps and the neighbours responses but little new had turned up and it had been a frustrating round of discussions.

'Uhm, again a consensus on all so far,' the Inspector interjected. 'Do not despair. Police work is not just about discovery it is also about corroboration and con-firmation; triangulation of information and eliminating lines of enquiry. We press on.'

He hid his disappointment that the hair sample was the only new lead to turn up so far but he knew this was a long-distance race and not a sprint. He remained confident that they would catch the culprit before or during the final lap. DC Chandler imagined the sce-nario. 'They shall not be the one to break the tape,' he whispered to himself.

13. The Salt King.
18th November 2022. (After)

We strolled hand in hand along the walkway that skirted up and away from the main A38 Birmingham to Worcester arterial road and reaches Avoncroft Museum on the South side of Bromsgrove. Passing the museum heading south we were in sight of the Bromsgrove Pre-Preparatory and Nursery School, formerly known as Stoke Grange.

'This is a great house,' said Clemmie. 'It is so steeped in industrial history Andrew. It was bought by local philanthropist John Corbett to be near his beloved Stoke Salt Works before he moved into the Chateau Impney for his equally beloved wife. In the 1930's it passed to George Cadbury who developed it into an adult education centre before the school took ownership in the early part of this century. What a lovely past it has.'

'I would buy it for you Clemmie if it was available,' I said with all the sincerity of a lovestruck puppy. 'Although I would have to explore how I can become a business man and philanthropist making money from the mining and manufacture of salt from salt beds whilst making sure the town folk benefitted from the development of brine baths and hotels.'

She laughed as we walked on past the cricket ground and headed for a bridleway that would take us to our canal pub destination.

'You're my Salt King Andrew wherever we are,' she said squeezing my arm. 'I already have a part of a big house and I don't need that as much as I need you.' Our pace slowed as my heart swelled with love for her in the silent moments that followed.

I took my time. We had neither cemented our arrangement, or consummated our relationship through sexual intimacy in the evening of our last meeting but it was wonderful to hear her talk in these tones. I reciprocated.

'Clemmie, I need you too. Ours has been a slow burner I know. We have been aware of each other for a while now and I beg to suggest that I have not recognised or even contemplated how I feel until now. Do you sisters know of our liaison?'

'I have not shared that yet but I feel that they know something has changed for me. There is something instinctive and deep rooted between us. We almost know each other's thoughts. I will tell them and it will be soon but just give me time.'

'That's fine with me but don't take too long, otherwise our dalliance the other day will be out. Someone either of us might know must have seen us outside the bank. It is inconceivable in such a community as ours.' Further contemplative silence followed by which time our feet had led us to St Michaels Church and the route through the well-preserved graveyard.

'Another Corbett reference,' I said, not wanting to change the subject but feeling I should and knowing that she was enjoying the topic. 'His grave currently sitting here is strangely re-assuring and he must be smiling from above now, looking down on his own John Corbett Way.'

Stretching from Droitwich and passing his former stately home of the Chateau Impney, we meandered down Corbett Way all the way to Bromsgrove and considered it a fitting memorial for a major local industrial figure of his time. Under him the Stoke Prior salt works had become the largest in Europe with an impressive annual tonnage. It was not difficult to imagine the commitment in time and energy needed to make all that a reality.

'One should not assume he is looking down,' was her casual witty retort and we shared a soft chuckle together.

The past was never lost on us and our shared interest and our passion for local history was palpable. It had helped in forming our bond of friendship. We walked on both comfortable and relaxed in each other's company, enjoying the simple pleasures of life.

14. Swipe Left. 20th June 2022. (Before)

Lickey was lounging back in her chair, her legs over the arm and her mobile phone in her hand scrolling though eligible men once again. She was familiar with and knew her way around the sites she was scrolling and surfing through. She had been studying them diligently over recent weeks; very important to look at the picture first as it was no good if she didn't find them attractive. Look at their profession; no lack of intellect allowed and ambition essential. Then look at their interests; no real preference here but they had to have something that motivated them and showed a greater breadth of character on top of their work. After that, a meeting sometimes resulted to disprove all that she had believed to be true and sometimes if she saw a spark, a second date. She had not lost faith in the process yet but the right one had not appeared so far. Coffee shops, early evening bars, event arenas and sporting occasions had all been and gone. She couldn't say that she hadn't enjoyed many of those liaisons but a man of substance who could look after her had not emerged yet.

Her two-year long relationship with Bartholomew had come to end during the Easter period of 2022 and she had struggled to come to terms with the vacuum that had been created in her life. Lickey thought she had chosen the right man and she had not wanted it to end the way it did. Whilst she had fought a restless battle with her feelings, she did harbour some animosity towards him and the sense of rejection was still palpable. She had been in the wrong and had broken his trust and yes she had let him down but she had been honest and apologetic and regretful. Lickey could not keep her brief affair a secret and she had opened up to him; had confided in him trusting that he would forgive her. She had shared her most intimate secrets and world views and had expected to grow a life together. She had once even contemplated marriage and a possibility of children but had recognised a lack of strength in him through his reaction to her indiscretion. Now these thoughts were shattered and though she had always considered herself a strong independent woman her limits were being stretched. She knew also that deep down it was all her fault.

It was another failure in her life. She had had so much young promise, doing very well at school, destined to become a doctor but she had found the challenge of a Biochemistry degree too much and gave up during her second year. Her parents were disappointed of course and wanted her to take the advice suggested by Kings University and follow one pure science degree. She had always been top of her year in Biology at school but she was adamant she wanted to drop out and come home. London she said didn't suit her. Despite the disappointment, her parents welcomed her home and tried to encourage her but she had flip flopped from one career idea to the next without real conviction. 'Only the lot of the too comfortable,' her father would say and she knew what he meant.

Her deep dive into the internet world of dating had not yielded the rewards she sought and disappointment was etched on her face. There was some anger there and this was tinged with frustration. She was used to getting what she wanted. Her father had showered her with high expectations mainly through giving her what she wanted when she wanted it. It was proving to be a poison chalice. She denied accusations that she was spoilt but would accept she had a demanding nature and enjoyed the very best. That is one of the reasons why she could never see eye to eye with Maximillian although she seemed overtly saddened by the news of his death. Max had told her he 'saw through her' and 'recognised a shallowness in her.' She had not appreciated that. Nevertheless, she had used the phrase 'Too young too soon,' to all that had asked.

She was losing patience. For the last hour she had been swiping left to reject men on the screen. There must be better ways to find a guy rather than this futile wate of time. She was not short on confidence and knew she was an attractive woman. With immaculately groomed long straight blond hair, gentle light blue eyes and a delicate nose she was the picture of elegance and gentle English sophistication. She had always believed that to be the case and had been assured many times over if this. She was slim and wore understated clothes that reflected a charming elegance rather than a stunning distinction. Her demeanour shrouded a steely desire to get what she wanted and she didn't take kindly to rejection and had never understood nor reflected on why she lacked a queue of willing suitors. She closed down the screen and threw the 'phone down lazily onto the sofa opposite. It bounced and fell to the floor and she left it there uncaringly.

This was not how she envisaged her life. She knew she was a beautiful woman with a wide range of personal qualities, perhaps a little head strong but men should have been lining up. What possessed her to become nothing more than a perfidious lover? She thought of Bart. Loving, caring Bart. He would do anything for her despite his weaknesses. Perhaps her motivations had been confused and she had lost sight of his good intentions. She resolved to get in touch with him and had the audacity to believe he would open his arms to her again given the time to reflect. She was right.

15. The Christmas Gathering.
15th December 2022. (After)

Bromsgrove town is the epicentre of the Bromsgrove district that includes Hagley and Rubery to the north, Dodford to the west, Stoke Prior to the south and Alvechurch and Tardebigge to the east. It's place names include such rolling tongue softeners such as Coften Hackett, Belbroughton, Romsley Top and Rowney Green. It also has some locations whose names are somewhat less appealing and whose adoption lie within the responsibilities of town planners and town or parish councils through the years. One can only assume that these esteemed custodians lacked imagination, were worse for wear or held a roguish tongue in cheek when they voted to pass through Bumble Hole Lane, Peters Finger, Bell End and Lickey End as locations.

If you follow Bumble Hole Lane up to its meeting with Valley Road you will eventually get to Bourneheath which among a number of local hostelries lies the Nailers Arms; a hark back to the past of one of Bromsgrove's main manufacturing industries in the eighteenth and nineteenth century. It was here in the restaurant that the Christmas gathering of the Collectors Club was taking place. The group had enjoyed a seasonal lunch after which the meeting took on a more formal accent. Sangita Kumar was holding the floor with a short presentation on art in the modern age.

'So, art now is not so much about being dead before you are famous or rich. It is not now about suffering for your art or relying on a benefactor. Today is about making a name and making sure your worth is recognised. Look at the number of musicians now selling their life work to streaming giants, artists selling their work for millions on the internet and writers striking massive deals before publication and not waiting for royalties to trickle in for their heirs…..'

'It's true you know, what she says,' whispered Elise quietly to Lamont from the other end of the table. 'The old image of struggling masters has gone to be replaced by a much more aggressive, bold more worldly artists. Look at Hirst, Hockney, Gormley – all relatively well off in their later life and well-funded from sales or commissions.'

Lamont leant back in his chair to reply conscious of any perceived ill manners whilst Sangita rounded up her presentation.

'Yes, some but not all. There are still many who strive and suffer,' he said. 'It is in the beauty of art that makes it reason enough to pursue.' A cheeky grin widened across his face. 'I was educated to believe that all artists 'suffer' in different ways for their art through either madness, ill-health or relationships. I suppose I will have to get used to this new reality. *Arts for art sake money for god's sake* sung 10CC.' Lamont was enjoying his own insights a little too much.

Sangita finished her presentation with a remarkable coincidence of thought.

'…and I conclude,' she said passionately, 'that far from promoting the body of thought that believes art should have no other aim than art itself I propose that art has always had a greater value to society. It is not a self-indulgent pastime free from moral, social or political norms but now has both an aesthetical and monetary value to the creator and their audience at the time of their creation and beyond.'

A ripple of applause resounded around the table and she took a shallow bow whilst wearing a broad smile of appreciation. I couldn't help the indulgence in thinking that a little bit of that was reserved for me. The room broke into enthusiastic conversation.

Elise continued her discourse with Lamont. 'I've never seen Sangita looking so radiant. She exuded a warmth and confidence that does her great credit. She should take her own advice and sell a small proportion of her collection. She certainly needs to.' As the words left her mouth she realised she had spoken out of turn.

'What do you mean by that?'

'Oh nothing. I think I've already said too many words in the wrong order already dear.'

Lamont looked around the room seemingly moving on but registering the comment. He looked at Andrew and thought how well he had done to establish the society. It was lively, informative and socially constructive. It was a regular opportunity to let friends see each other with a probably unique focus. He didn't miss Maximillian though. He was an unfortunate sidebar to a much more interesting story. Always stirring a troublesome cake and watching others eat it, Lamont could not understand his motives and now that he has gone for good he never would. He smiled as he thought of the work that he'd picked up since the society had been formed. Word of mouth was such a good thing and his friends had been kind to him both here and through the Court Leet. He felt very much at home in an agreeable network of friends. 'Now why does Elise think that Sangita needs to sell off some of her art collection?' he reflected.

Clemmie smiled lovingly across the table towards me. I returned the gesture. She was sat with her sisters as usual, which in the context of the meeting, I didn't mind but I couldn't wait to have her by my side again. Things were going very well in that department and although our relationship had not been publicised it was no longer a secret. Her sisters had taken it very well considering their history together and although surprised they had been very accepting and happy for their sibling. This was not a consequence of the collector's society that I had been expecting nor planning and I was doubly thankful for the direction of travel it had taken.

The presentation on art now over, the group mingled around the room some leaving their seats for alternative sources of conversation. Sassy ambled gracefully over in my direction. I had noticed a slight shift in her demeanour since the tragic death of Maximillian at the start of November; although events had affected us all Sassy had caried a sense of unease with her since then.

'Another good evening Andrew. You should be proud of yourself. The society goes from strength to strength!'

'Thank you Sassy. I appreciate that. You are of course important going forward as a founder member. Its future very much depends on the likes of you'.

Sassy stared across the room.

'And where now Andrew?'

'Oh let's get this gathering over with first,' I said.

'No silly, you're teasing. I mean with my sister.'

I thought she was being intrusive but I hid my annoyance. I knew this was something I had to factor into my relationship if it was going to survive. Without giving too much away about what I didn't know anyway I replied politely.

'One day at a time Sassy. We are very happy as we are at the moment.'

Looking across the room rather than directly at me came the reply with slightly sinister undertones, 'Don't hurt her Andrew.'

She moved away smiling at me over her shoulder and moved to talk to Bart without another word. I was disappointed with myself in not being sharp or quick enough with my reply but the moment had gone and I was not going to follow her across the room to further the conversation. Why would she say that? I was not that sort of person and certainly didn't have a dishonourable reputation as a notorious seducer. The more I thought about it the more anger I felt and I resolved to continue that discussion at a future date. It was not something that I wanted to even mention to Clemmie although if she found out from Sassy I knew it would crop up.

The evening was coming to a close and I drew the meeting to a conclusion by standing up, tapping on the side of an available glass with a tea spoon and asking all for their attention for a few minutes.

'Thank you all for coming and making the evening what it is.'

This brought a gentle ripple of applause and I continued with the short eulogy to Max that I had promised myself. I watched as some in the audience bowed their heads as if in prayer, others stared onto space and others stared right at me. They were all without exception respectfully observant. After a silent moment of reflection on his life I continued.

125

'...... and now to conclude; at the end of the last meeting I consulted a few people on where we might go with our little soiree. I have taken the liberty of taking a preliminary booking of the Parkside Suite in town for an 'open house' session. This would be for collectors and other interested parties who may wish to look over our hoards and for us to share knowledge and understanding in our chosen fields. I feel I must say though that the cost of renting a suitable space for larger numbers goes into the hundreds of pounds so I ask if we are all prepared to put in twenty pounds to cover such a venture'.

I looked around the room. There were neither dissenting voices nor disgruntled looks, only nods of encouragement. I smiled in acknowledgement.

'Of course,' I said, 'if anyone changes their mind I will seek to cover the deficit so that the evening can go ahead.' I knew there was a small risk in suggesting this but I also knew that by the announcement it would pull a few chords and I wanted to show Clemmie that I meant business too. 'I will circulate the date when I have confirmed the booking.'

The room broke into spontaneous conversation that I didn't want to interrupt further and I took my seat as an indication that I had finished.

16. A Surprising Find.
14th February 2022. (Before)

Lamont was listening to Byonce's song 'Irreplaceable' from her 2006 album B'Day. It was his favourite from her earlier works and he enjoyed singing along to it. It was a contrast to some of her music that he used during his training sessions that had a more strident, stronger beat and faster tempo. Those pieces were ready made for workouts and he was eternally grateful for her music.

He had given himself the day off by keeping his diary free but in reality all it meant was that he caught up with essential admin or 'sadmin' as he sometimes called it. Whilst working for oneself carried many benefits there were a number of very specific drawbacks. Keeping a detailed diary, preparing bespoke classes, servicing invoices and receipts, expenses and tax returns, promotions and advertising to name but a few. Today he had decided to file his receipts, payments and expenses. Despite the many electronic means at his disposal, he still kept an important box into which he places all documents when he got them and devoted the time to sorting them out once a month. It was a routine job and one that sometimes allowed his mind to wander. It was a responsibility that usually took him a couple of hours and although he never relished starting it, he always felt cathartically cleansed when he had finished. He had the internet banking on his laptop screen open, easily checking receipts against payments and kept a running total of incidental expenditure. As a sole trader he knew the inland revenue were always lurking round the corner and he was diligent in keeping his affairs in order.

He had been sitting at his desk for approximately an hour when he opened an envelope from Sassy Cartwright. It contained a cheque for all his work with the girls in January. He smiled. It always amused him that not only did the girls pay and play as one, leaving the administration to Sassy, but that they paid by cheque when there was so many easier ways to pay. I thought they ran a software start-up he whispered ruefully. Lamont drew the cheque out of the envelope and noticed a small slip of paper float to the floor. He reached down and picked it up. He unfolded the doubled paper; *'You are not my keeper, leave me alone,'* it read.

'What is this?' he said aloud in surprise. Lamont sat back and with a pensive stare though the window of his study, he stretched both arms behind his head and stroked his muscular neck. 'This can't be for me,' he thought. Knowing that it was not unusual for Sassy to leave a short note of thanks with payment he quickly resolved to speak with her at the earliest opportunity. Clearly a mistake had been made hadn't it? He decided that the note may have been personal and he shouldn't intrude and certainly not involve the other girls. Then he wondered if he had at some point over stepped the mark. Had she picked up that he found her attractive? He tried to re-trace his movements, actions and words in her presence but it was an insurmountable task. He felt unsure whether Sassy was going to feel some embarrassment and unease regarding this apparent error but it would be wrong to ignore it. Looking in his diary, he saw a booking for the girls the day after tomorrow. He would take her aside for a private chat after the session citing an administrative matter he decided.

⟫ ⟪

After further thought Lamont decided to call Sassy and arrange a private meet up. He thought that, out of the alternatives, this would be better that taking her aside when the other girls were there. 'More room for honesty and frankness,' he thought.

He met Sassy on the eighteenth of February at The Talbot a country pub and restaurant in the village of Belbroughton. The village lay on the lower slopes of the Clent Hills about six miles north of Bromsgrove. They had chosen to meet here for its proximity and its distance. Not too far to be inconvenient but far enough to be confidential. Not that Lamont needed it. He had reasonable deniability of any liaison though the note in his pocket suggested some form of impropriety. Sassy had arrived and found him waiting by the bar with a pint of lager in his hand. He noticed her entrance and stood up politely to greet her with a kiss on the cheek. He noticed that she accepted gracefully and this put him at ease.

'What would you like to drink Sassy?'

'Oh a raspberry gin and ginger ale would be lovely thanks.'

Whilst Lamont waited to the bar she found a table she liked, opened her Mulberry handbag and drew out her lipstick to freshen up and checked her face in the compact mirror she carried routinely.

Lamont returned with her drink and placed it carefully on their table whilst ensuring eye contact.

'Delicately sweet – just like you,' he thought, wary not to expose his inner words.

'Lamont I was pleased to get your call but what is it that can't be discussed over the phone or was that just a ruse to get me here?' she asked.

'All of the above,' Lamont replied with a gentle smile rising on his lips and entering his eyes.

'I really wanted to meet with you for your company but also for something I came across in something from you that surprised me.' He dropped his hand into his back pocket, withdrew his wallet and pulled out the slip of paper that read

'You are not my keeper leave me alone.'

He opened it and slowly pushed it across the table.

Sassy blanched. She knew what it was straight away but how did it end up with him? A realisation crossed her face and her embarrassment showed. She had no intention of creating an alternative narrative where she might dig herself into a rabbit warren of lies.

Lamont saw her unease. 'Sassy you don't have to explain unless it relates to me. If it's just a mistake and it somehow just ended up in the wrong place please just say so. I don't want to pry.'

'I certainly think a mistake has been made Lamont and I apologise for that. I would never write something like this to you. I prize our friendship too highly. I am embarrassed. Would you mind confirming how you got hold of this?'

'Of course. It was in a payment receipt envelope that you sent me. I opened it and this note just fell out.'

'As I thought. Oh gosh what an idiot!' exclaimed Sassy.

Lamont looked deflated.

'No sorry, not you Lamont; me. I'm the idiot on so many levels.' said Sassy.

Brightening up he replied 'Oh no Sassy you couldn't be an idiot if you tried. Is there anything I can do to help the situation?'

Sassy thought for a moment and then her story cascaded from her lips. Lamont listened intently. Of all the things he thought it might have been this was not what he was expecting

Her attraction to Max, the dating and the short four-week relationship. The quickly developing control and coercion of her life and the increasingly threatening nature of his behaviour towards her. She would not accept it and had not been raised to be treated like this.

Perhaps she was over reacting but she was a strong independent woman and she would arrange her life as she saw fit. She would go where she wanted and see who she likes and he would not stop her. He had struck her hard across the face and made her lip bleed. That was it. 'Get out' she had screamed pushing him on the chest with both hands and shoving him toward the door. He had gone, thank goodness. She had not been ready for his refusal to leave had it happened. The house had been empty and there would have been no one there to help her. Her sisters knew nothing. She could have reported him she knew – and probably should have – but wanted to put the whole episode behind her and get on with her life. She didn't consider herself in danger but he was still bothering her with angry telephone calls and surreptitious menacing and hostile looks when in company. She ignored him but she was irritated by his behaviour.

The note had been an attempt to finish it completely but her failure to send it meant that the message had not been given and he was still persisting. She realised that now. It was not at a level that she could not handle but he was a lamentable fool if he thought he could treat her like that and get away with it. It was over and there was no going back.

135

Lamont looked shocked and angry and the smouldering ire he held for Max simmered to the surface. He knew Max's behaviour was unacceptable by any standards but why was he so surprised? He already held a long-standing negative view of him but had supressed it for the sake of his friendship with others. Now the gloves were off.

'How can I help?' he had asked and Sassy told him.

>>>- <<<

Not wanting to leave Sassy disappointed he had pledged to himself that he would act quickly. The situation required a cool head and his interactions with Max were already inflamed. He disliked Max deeply but where would he get the cold water from to bring the temperature down he pondered? His mind was whirring for an answer. Andrew Byron he thought. This is a job for him. A skilful arbiter, a trusted friend and a professional negotiator. Wait he thought, Sassy entrusted me. Would she accept others knowing of her predicament. But then Andrew was nothing if not a person you could confide in and know that it would go no further.

Of course, there was a risk. He was a good friend to Max and that may influence him but he was fond of the triplets too and wouldn't countenance someone hurting any of them. For goodness sake they have had enough hurt in their lives. He resolved to speak to Andrew, confident that he would be able to help. He picked up his phone and they arranged to meet the following day

⋙ ⋘

I met Lamont at the back of the church nave on the 20th February. It seemed like a strange place to choose but he wanted somewhere private. I had left the office to meet him during my break so needed somewhere close by. I picked up the anxiety in his voice and a desire to meet and it appeared like a suitable place for a private conversation. He was already seated when I arrived so I approached quietly and sat down on the pew next to him. He appeared to be sat praying but turned his neck as he felt my presence.

'Hello Lamont, are you OK?'

'I am but Sassy isn't,' he said getting straight to the point.

The hairs on my neck bristled with anticipation tinged with, on hearing that name, a could not help myself feel a morsel of mistrust.

'What's the matter with her?' I said anxiously. He went on to tell me the same sorry tale that Sassy had narrated to him the day before.

'Now here I am Andrew, seeking your advice and guidance because I don't know what to do for the best. I know what I want to do to Max but I don't think that will help Sassy at all and it is she that is uttermost in my mind right now.'

My friend Max. My cross to bear. Always saving him, always supporting him, always having his back. I had to admit to myself I was running out of patience with his inability to learn from his mistakes over the years. He had regularly failed to transfer the social subtleties I had tried to help him with into different situations. Now another friend was being hurt by his actions as well as the ripple effect to others. Perhaps I had been exercising blind loyalty too long. Maybe I should have ditched him as a bad lot years ago but I was not built like that. I prized loyalty and always had. Walking away was not my style. Whilst knowing that Lamont was seeking a fast resolution for his friend I needed time to think and told him that. There were always two sides to a tale.

'Time Andrew?' he whispered with frustration. 'She needs action. What can I do now?'

'I actually don't think you should do anything Lamont that you would repent later. You know I know Max well and I do want to help because you've asked me to. Leave it with me for twenty-four hours and I'll let you know what I propose and we'll talk it over then.'

'I trust your judgement Andrew. I shall contain myself begrudgingly for another day before I rip his head off.'

'Whatever, I shall not be recommending that course of action,' I said forcing a smile. 'Promise me that you will not do anything rash.'

He nodded in reluctant acquiescence.

We left the church as we entered it; quietly and solemnly. It had not been a religious visit and I didn't want to draw attention to that fact.

We shook hands. 'Look Andrew I trust you and will rely on your advice. At the very least I have un-burdened myself and taken a weight off my shoulders for a while. The true burden however, lies with Sassy and I can't countenance it for long. Good bye my friend and I'll speak to you tomorrow'

Continuing to hold onto his hand I placed my other palm across his large wrapped fist.

'I'll try my best Lamont. You know I will.'

Lamont headed for the car park close to my offices and I headed to the graveyard to a bit of quiet space to think.

'You and your good reputation,' I thought to myself. 'Carrying other people's weight is not a blessing.'

I lifted my chin, turned up my collar to the wind and strode purposefully and pensively in the winter sunshine. '...but helping is what you do best,' said a voice in my brain.

I thought about Sassy a lot that afternoon. Her confidence, her assurance and her charismatic air. She drew people into her orbit and made them circle there naturally.

I thought about Max too; Max the chameleon, Max the competitor, Max the perfectionist, Max the buffoon and Max the philanderer. Max the all-round gregarious 'good egg' in the club bar and the ale houses around the town; particularly, it had to be said, in predominantly in male company. Some would say he was an opportunist and a player. Perhaps I was missing something, a darker side perhaps? But then there are always two sides to any story and often more than that;

I should hear him out. I allowed my mind to wander further. What if my belief in the best of people was letting me down and blinding me to the truth behind the man?

17. The Deal. 29th January 2021 (Before)

The Garrington factory was well known in Bromsgrove during the nineteen sixties and seventies as a supplier of car parts to the massive but ultimately doomed Longbridge car production line, a ten-minute drive away. A significant housing development had now replaced it and in a small enclosed area housing a statue commemorating the towns industrial and engineering past, an animated Bart Bramble sat facing Max Charles. It was a grey day and they were both shrouded in a heavy mist that suited them both. Bart looked around anxiously whilst trying to disguise a nervous twitch on the left side of his mouth. Despite his coat, scarf and gloves he felt an involuntary shiver. Had anyone been peering through the mist their view would have been obscured and they would not have been able to suppose the conversation.

'Listen Max, I may have done this once before for you – and I know I owe you – but I cannot and will not become your long-term dealer. I am being drawn into a situation that I am completely uncomfortable with, not least of all because I consider you a friend.'

'I scratch your back and you scratch mine dear Bart. If I say I need you right now I don't expect you to let me down,' replied Max casting a suspicious glance from side to side and around into nowhere. 'We are compatriots and brothers in arms and I *Primus inter pares*, first amongst equals, leader of men.'

'Don't play the guilt card on me now. This is wrong on so many levels. Your habit, my involvement, your guilt tripping me and your predated philosophy from antiquity. It won't work anymore.'

'No, no, no,' said Max. 'No guilt trip......this is what you owe me. We all have our secrets don't we Bart and we all have to pay up for them sooner or later. If you don't want me to service your gambling debt any longer I can just call it in. Just let me know. On the other hand, if you can't pay me cash, well there are other options available to balance my book with you and this is one of them.'

Bart jumped to his feet clearly holding back his anger. It was a convincing display from a usually mild-mannered man. He knew his position was perilous but he grew up believing that without his principles he was nothing. He felt compromised but summoned the strength to take up an aggressive pose. Pushing his face almost to the point of touching Max's nose Bart slowly spelt out his message hissing decidedly. 'I … have… nothing … to … say … and … will … have … nothing … to … do … with … this.' He continued to stare into the eyes of his apparent nemesis before turning and striding quickly away.

'Oh I think you will my friend, I think you will,' came the gentle whisper into the stillness of the evening gloom from an unruffled Maximillian Charles.

18. The Agenda for the Meeting. 5th January 2023. (After)

'Thanks for being here. There is only one agenda for this meeting and that is to strengthen our position in relation to where we are in the case of Maximilian Charles.'

The detective was brisk and business like. He carried the air of someone who wanted and needed to get moving. They had been treading water long enough. They sat in a triangular shape all facing each other.

'Anthony what have you got for me?'

'Well gov quite a lot really. First I went to the morgue again and spoke to the pathologist. He went into some detail regarding the facial injuries and he thinks that many of them were induced by the car accident itself but that the frontal head injuries were caused by a smashing of the nose into the steering wheel by someone holding the victims hair and pulling the head forcibly forward. This is indicated through a transparent swelling of the root called the bulb, the size of the hair bulb and areas of bleeding around the root of the follicle. Certainly once, possibly twice. The next bit of news could be a game changer though. He also thinks that Max Charles was a drug user. There are marks on his forearm that suggest injection.'

'For God's sake why didn't they tell us this before now?' shouted Chandler. 'We already knew that narcotics were present at the scene. I'm not happy about that.'

He calmed himself, frustrated at the apparent oversight and annoyed with himself for not pursuing it in the first place. 'This opens up a whole new line of questioning. If he's injecting someone will know. We need to find that someone and find the something that they're hiding.'

He noted this find on a post-it note and added it to the mood board. He liked corroboration but he liked revelation better . 'Go on Anthony, what else have you got?'

'The constable of the Bromsgrove Court Leet is called a petty constable and is not a real constable as we understand it. Nevertheless, his name is Richard Proudlove, a prominent DIY shop owner in the town. He was very happy to help us and could not praise Elise Goodrich enough. She, in turn, only had good words to say about Andrew Bryant. He also likes Lamont Adams but stressed that Lamont's relationship with Max Charles was strained and their views often collided during meetings. He said their antipathy towards each other was not a secret. They both had a strong presence and could both be physically intimidating. He saw all three as very good friends but viewed Elise as the galvanising force amongst them. Simone did the rest.'

Anthony Black turned his eyes towards Simone as if in a silent pre-agreed pact. Simone picked up the thread.

'Yes Guv, I went to speak to Lickey Farrier. She's not an easy one to read and very deliberate and wary in her answers. She admitted that she found Max Charles difficult and annoying but at times charming and friendly. She re-iterated that she was at home on the night of his murder and the 'phone call from Bart Bramble is substantiated through phone records although the time of the call doesn't mean she wasn't out earlier.'

'Had you used the word murder Simone?' interjected Chandler.

Simone studied her note book and chewed the end of her pen.

'No Guv, she was the one to use it.'

'Interesting,' he whispered pensively. 'Go on.'

'One thing of interest I think you might like to know is that on the book shelf of Lickey Farrier's study is a copy of the Stanley Gibbons catalogue.'

DI Chandler sat up straight. Anthony Black looked on in confusion.

'That Anthony, is the stamp collector's bible for many; and our first real clue of potential deceit.' said his boss. 'Thanks for that awareness. You take today's prize Simone.'

Simone smiled and continued, well aware that there was no prize other than Chandler's appreciation, which was more than enough for her.

'No surprises door to door. Neighbours wanted to be helpful and no conflicting reports, only supporting current evidence. There was a report from Chaddesley Corbett of some loud revving of an engine about midnight on the night in question but that's not unusual and they didn't think to look out of the window.'

Chandler stood and stared out of his window. His thoughts were racing. Two great leads today. Sometimes nothing then at other times a great deal. 'What are you hiding that we need to know from you Lickey?' he said out loud but out of earshot of his lieutenants.

He silently reminded himself to pay Ms Locket further attention but first he needed to know who knew about the drug habit of the victim and why they were hiding it?

19. The Rebuff.
14th February 2022. (Before)

On the evening of the day that Lamont had found out about Sassy's dalliance with Maximillian the triplets held a small party of friends for Valentine' day.

The kiss lasted longer than it should have. There was a guilty pleasure on both parts and Lickey knew it. She gently pulled away. How can this be happening when I love my partner? Then lost in the moment she drew her lips up to him for more. Max curled his strong arms around her squeezing her to the point of suffocation and tasting her lips with added urgency; suddenly unleashing his desire he thrust his torso against her and she felt his lust. He moved his hand to cup her breast....

No! Placing two hands over his chest Lickey pushed away and ran down the stairs, adjusting her clothes and hair and back into the party. There was plenty of familiar faces but drinks were aplenty and spirits were high. No one, she had thought, took any notice of the forced smile on her innocent face as she mingled seemingly effortlessly.

The evening came to a natural end as guests took their well-mannered leave. Bartholomew gathered up her coat and gently guided her arms into its sleeves and over her shoulders. Looking back, Lickey gave a soft blue-eyed glance of thanks and lifted her long straight blonde hair over the collar.

'Thanks for a really good evening girls', said Bart, as Ora, Clemmie and Sassy looked on. 'My little valentine and I really enjoyed it.'

'Yes, *we* certainly did.' thought Lickey.

Max sauntered over to be with the departing crowd. 'Yes, a lovely evening and so glad I was able to squeeze it in,' briefly meeting Lickey's gaze without arousing suspicion. Lickey felt a frisson of pleasure and had to suppress her excitement.

'Oh, it was no trouble and thanks for coming,' said Clemmie. 'It's nice to celebrate Valentine's night with friends even when there's no room for Mr Valentine himself,' added Ora. Sassy looked over at Bart with a smile as if in silent conversation. Car engines started, rev counters were engaged and motors pulsed as waves and shouts of appreciation filled the night sky and exhaust fumes disappeared as quickly as the cars sped from view.

Bart circled his left arm around Lickey's car seat and kissed her lightly on the head.

'That was a lovely night. Let's not end it there when we get to yours. You're looking gorgeous.'

'Let's leave it tonight Bart. I'm very tired and I have a head ache from the red wine,' she said.

She had been in a relationship with Bart now for nearly two years. They were happy and content in each other's company. Neither of them had challenged the depth of their love until this moment and whilst Lickey had always fancied Max from her school days she never thought of a real encounter that would manifest her school girl thoughts. Her feelings were confused and she wondered what Max was thinking at the time but more important now.

'What have I done?' she thought in secret pleasure and without a hint of regret.

Bart looked disappointed but did not argue. He gave her a look that Lickey couldn't quite interpret. The remainder of the twenty-five-minute journey from Hanbury to the Lickey Hills was quiet apart from late night Classic FM as Bart took the cross-country route to Hewell Grange. 'I'm not going to get locked up for that man' he thought as they passed the prison entrance on his right.

They arrived and parked up. Neither made the move to get out of the car.

'Are you sure about tonight?'

'Yes, I'm sorry.'

She leant over and kissed him on the lips. A loving and real kiss that re-assured him.

'Very well. I'll ring you in the morning to see how you are. I love you.'

'I love you too.'

She reached for the door handle and swung herself out of the seat quickly fumbling awkwardly for her house keys as she waved him off. He suddenly became aware of the increasing physical distance between them. Is this a metaphor for something else? Recently little things had changed. I don't want to lose her too he thought as he drove off.

20. Pride Comes Before a Fall.
16th February 2022 (Before)

I drove over to see Max in the early evening of the sixteenth of February. It was a Wednesday and I remember the date because it was his birthday and he was apparently 'going out at eight'. It was not a good time but I had to have it out with him. I reasoned it was for his own good as his reputation was being sullied; as well as the obvious hurt and damage being done to Sassy, not to mention Lamont's anger. He thought I was just going round with a gift and I would have had to believe in extreme altruism to think that that was the case.

He welcomed me at the door and I followed him inside. I accepted the offer of a drink and had a small bottled beer in consideration of my driving. Not that Max paid too much attention to that. Despite repeated warnings he would down three drinks even when he was using his car citing a strong metabolism, the time over which he drunk and the quiet roads he travelled on. His intransigence was well known and those around him had stopped trying to convince him otherwise.

I handed him a small gift box containing a model of his Maserati GranTorismo and he received it warmly. It was a safe steer on my part but I think he appreciated it. I didn't take long to broach the topic I had come to discuss. I think he was genuinely shocked but quickly became defensive.

'What's it got to do with Lamont, the bastard?' he shouted. His response had been predictable.

I knew Lamont's name would spark a fire but I couldn't leave it out.

'Max, this isn't about Lamont but how you have treat and continue to treat Sassy.'

'Oh she's over reacting Andrew. You know how emotional women can be. Anyway, I don't care. If she wants to play it this way I'll have nothing more to do with her. She's a Prima Donna; a raging nut case full of pretentious arrogance and a dislike of men. She was always demeaning towards me looking to shrink me by always disagreeing with my opinions and under-mining my beliefs.'

He was venting his spleen but I interrupted, breath-ing a half sigh of relief and ignoring the diatribe. 'Well, that would suit both of you then. Perhaps a period of silence between you would be the best thing to calm the senses and repair the nerves. It would be a shame to scar your relationship totally and perhaps in the long term you may able to be friends again.'

'There's no point. I didn't see her as a friend Andrew. She was an attractive date that's all. I have nothing in common with her and she has little to say to me that I could agree on. As for that festering lackey Lamont I'll deal with him separately.'

I felt the situation slipping away once again.

'No Max that's not a good idea. I have come in good faith to calm the waters and seek a resolution not to add fuel to the fire. You know I have always had your best interests at heart and supported you through thick and thin. Please don't let me down.'

This was a line that I had used before on him. Deep down he knew I was right. It was just hard getting to that underground place in him. A cessation in hostility was all I sought at this stage. Further antagonism or worse still, violence, could only lead to further damage and or a legal process that would result in more hurt, possible conviction and further resentment. I had to stop the snow ball rolling down the hill. I urged him to do as he suggested and avoid all contact until further

159

notice. I pleaded with him and he listened. At least I think he did.

Later that same evening I contacted Lamont. He wasn't that enamoured with what I told him but accepted that if further contact ceased between Max and Sassy he could live with that. He still wanted to 'batter his brains out' but could control the urge safe in the knowledge that Sassy was safe. He thanked me and asked me not to contact her and that he would see her and explain what action had been taken. I think he wanted to take some credit after all. I was happy for him to take it if that is what he wanted. In that sense I had been altruistic and I thought I had averted further confrontation. I was wrong on both counts.

21. Suspicion.
21st December 2022. (After)

Raymond Chandler sat at his desk pondering Maximillian Charles and the tragedy and mystery surrounding his death. On one level, a tragic accident and on the other a scientific mystery. Why would a mature man with some social standing and reputation take the risk of drug use before driving?

The case was perplexing him. Inspector Chandler had spent over twenty years in the police force. He had earned a reputation as a thorough and reliable investigator who always paid due diligence to his cases. He often told younger staff that 'all things were possible, fewer things were probable and one thing is probably actual' and that 'eliminating the many to reveal the few and eventually the one is the secret of good coppering. Time and patience, my friends, are the things that we must pride and treasure', he would add 'and are the very things that are often in less supply even from our leadership.'

He was schooled in Kipling and loved reciting the line,

'If you can keep your head whilst all around are losing theirs and blaming it on you.'

He stood up to stretch his long legs, leant over to pick up a pencil that had dropped on the floor and began spinning it through his fingers. Computers were there when you needed them but doodling and note taking was essential.

It was not hard to see why Raymond Chandler had risen through the ranks. A vastly experience officer of the West Mercian force he had completed his training and earned his spurs on foot patrol gaining a reputation of going the extra mile and closing cases. He applied for a position in the Criminal Investigation Department, well known as CID, because he was a divergent thinker, enjoyed criminal discovery and was found to have strengths in enquiry, interviewing and investigation. This role returned him to plain clothes, a switch that he appreciated, befitting his preference for a stylised appearance.

He was dressed in a royal blue suit, a white shirt, a blue tie of similar hue held in place by a gold tie pin, dark brown brogues and a matching colour belt. His tall poised demeanour was topped by a waft of light brown hair, swept back more by habit than design. He had a slim frame which in his defence he would argue that he didn't have much time to eat. In actuality he eat quite a lot through constant snacking while he thought.

He strode slowly around the room and reached for his note book stored in his inside breast pocket. This case was niggling him. Flicking over the pages he reached his list of interviews and re-read his summary of Andrew Byron's statement. He had been very frank and helpful. Almost too helpful. So, he was involved with Clemmie Cartwright who was the sister of both Sassy -who had been involved with the victim- and of Ora -who he claimed was jealous of that relationship. He also knew Bartholomew Bramble who was involved for some time with Lickey Farrier, who in turn was infatuated with the victim but who also despised him at intervals. Lamont Adams was also a friend and he had a poor relationship with the victim. There was a lot of weak motive *for* murder and no real evidence *of* murder.

A thorough forensic examination of the Morgan along with the other three cars in the collection had revealed little. The Morgan was certainly a mess but it had satisfied road worthiness and showed no evidence of brake tampering, sub-standard tyres, fuel problems or hydraulic failure. The other cars under the ownership of Max Charles would have equally satisfied all DVLA requirements for propriety. One could only assume that driver error was to blame in whatever form that blame accrued.

Then there was the property search that had revealed a sizable quantity of class A drugs and a number of small bags of marijuana together with a puzzling empty envelope addressed to Mr Charles with two unusual stamps left prominently on the desk; one with a quote taken form Shakespeare's King Lear *who is it that can tell me who I am* and a second depicting a skull and crossbones flag. Perhaps he was getting this wrong and this was a case of death through misadventure. On the other hand, the niggle had not gone away and he had come to trust that niggle.

Maybe I need another chat with our legal clerk he thought. He picked up his phone.

>>>- -<<<

Andrew had his mobile on silent but felt the vibration and answered.

164

Hello Andrew, it's Inspector Chandler. I was wondering if we could meet for another chat. We seem to be making progress on the Maximilian Charles case but I would like to explore a few more lines of enquiry with you as our last conversation was very useful.'

'Well I am at work at the moment Inspector but I can arrange to meet you later. Is six o'clock OK?' The Inspector's desire to glean more from me delighted and perplexed me in equal measure.

'That would be excellent. Can I come to you this time?' thinking it would be useful to see Andrew in his domestic setting.

'That suits me Inspector. I'll see you then.' My reticence for my neighbours to see a police car outside my house had subsided. The story was out and everyone who was networked into social media had already formed their mostly ridiculous far-fetched views.

'Thank you Andrew, I'll see you at six.'

With that done Chief Inspector Raymond Chandler put the phone down and immediately got to work on those lines of enquiry that he had spoken about.

Meanwhile I pressed the red button and cradled my phone in my hands. I thought I'd given him everything I knew and yet he wanted more from me. Where was this all going?

Raymond Chandler drove down the little cul-de-sac that was Peters Finger and carefully reversed into a tight parking space, taking care not to block anyone in or dent anyone's car. He was painfully aware of his social responsibility as a serving officer that his behaviour was tested above the standard that many apply to fellow citizens and he constantly reminded himself that criticism came quickly when one erred. He opened door, again carefully, put a large right foot down on the gravelly surface and strode purposefully but slowly towards the small terrace house. He gazed upwards towards the roof and down towards the door as if mentally painting a picture in his mind's eye. He knocked on the door.

'Welcome Inspector, please come in,' I said as I opened the door.

'Thank you.'

He very deliberately brushed his feet firmly against the door mat and took off his overcoat handing it over and onto my outstretched arm.

'Please, come through.'

I led him into a small sitting room, filled with what I thought was comfortable classical furniture knowing that it looked like it had passed the test of time. The open fire burned and the heat was palpable.

This is my snug inspector. It's where I retreat to on a cold winters evening when I have nothing else on.

'Take a seat please,' I said stretching out my other arm as a guide almost mirroring his hospitality when I visited Hindlip station.

'Would you like a drink of tea or coffee?'

'No, but thank you for offering. If you don't mind I'd like to get straight down to our business.'

'Very well.' I retreated to hang up the coat and returned taking a seat opposite him.

Pulling his well-worn note book from the breast pocket of his jacket the inspector fumbled for a pencil.

'Andrew you're a philatelist aren't you?'

'Yes that is right.'

'I wonder if you can help me with this.' He reached into his bag that he had placed beside him and pulled out a plastic cover with an envelope inside it. He removed the envelope and placed it on the coffee table between us. I looked at him.

'May I?'

'Of course.'

I picked it up turned it a couple of times in my fingers and looked inside. Nothing.

'Well the envelope is something that could be picked up in bulk in any stationary shop. The stamps are post the year two thousand. I'd say the one with the skull and crossbones is circa two thousand and one from a navy set of stamps and the other probably circa two thousand and eleven commemorating and celebrating the playwright William Shakespeare. They are unmarked that makes them a little bit more special but stuck on which reduces their worth even there is no post mark. The name and address is clear. It is a strange couple of stamps to use because of their different production dates and their value. They amount to far too much for a letter unless something of weight was inside and the postal service was never used anyway according to the lack of a cancellation mark.'

I passed the envelope safely back into his possession and he received it carefully placing it back into the plastic wallet and into his bag.

'Thank you. You have helped me greatly in establishing a number of issues I had with that envelope and now I have more. I will share with you that there is no evidence of a letter that I have found. It could have been torn and thrown away or burnt but let us assume for a moment one thing.' He paused. 'What if there was no letter?'

'What do you mean Inspector?'

'What if the sender's message was on the outside of the envelope and the message is in the stamps?'

I looked again.

'Who is it that can tell me who I am?' I read. Then, skull and crossbones, a signature of death. I gasped at the implication. Is he suggesting this a sinister message from someone intent on harm? He looked up and held an inviting stare. The Inspector was holding a fixed gaze as if to say 'what do you think' that made me feel uncomfortable. 'Does he think **I** may have something to do with this,' I thought.

I broke the long silence. 'This is cryptic Inspector but as you say is a possibility. There has certainly been some thought in the stamps applied and the absence of a letter is also suggestive.'

The Inspector rubbed his chin. 'Tell me Andrew who would have access to stamps of these dates?'

'Well any collector of British stamps would probably have these in their collection. That is, if they were bought and kept in mint condition or as part of a presentation pack. First day covers are stuck and cancelled on an envelope and so would not be available to use. Interestingly by January 2023 any personal store of stamps have to be used because of digitalisation or traded as a swap out for a barcoded version with the Royal Mail by March.'

'So what you are saying is that it is unlikely that someone would have thought of putting this threat together on the spur of the moment. This sort of symbolism, if that is what it is, would have been planned for a period of time in years, not months or days?'

'Well in theory yes but if someone wanted to they could access those stamps in many other ways.'

'How?'

'Steal them, trade them or raid their own collection,' I replied. Following a short reflective silence I went on.

'Inspector, just a thought. If those stamps were stuck on by hand would you not be able to take a thumb or finger print from them? Or even DNA the saliva on the back? Mind you, I can't remember if they were self-adhesive products.'

'Yes you're right Andrew but I've already been there. Those stamps are clean. Whoever put them on knew what they were doing.'

Inspector Raymond Chandler stood up and brushed down the creases in his trousers. 'Andrew I am most grateful for this discussion. It has been both enlightening and useful and now I must take my leave,' he said offering a hand of gratitude.

'Thank you Inspector,' I couldn't contain myself any longer and without any further consideration I said in a low and insistent voice, 'I hope you don't think that because I have a good working knowledge of stamps that I could somehow be mixed up in this?'

A gentle smile rose across his face that was both encouraging yet non-committal.

'Andrew, you must know that I cannot rule anything out until I have ruled something else in. The whole process is about eliminating the false to elucidate the true. I will say that at the moment you are not a direct line of enquiry but are a primary source of information that will progress this investigation. To date you have been very co-operative and helpful. I appreciate your support and the open way that you have engaged in our discussions. I hope that can continue.'

'I have nothing to hide inspector. I can tell you I do possess both of the stamps you have shown me today and would be happy to share them with you now.'

He held the step that he had made towards his coat and turned wistfully.

'Yes Andrew, I think that would be an excellent idea,' he said. I led him into the small parlour area that

I called my study and pulled out a box containing all my post millennium presentation packs. What if those two stamps ae not there I suddenly thought... too late now. I felt my pulse beating in my temple as I took off the lid and filed though to 2001. There in April was the pack still complete with the stamp of the 'jolly roger' in the 'flags and ensign' series. I breather an audible sigh of relief that was not lost on the Inspector. I passed the pack to him and he scanned it with genuine interest.

'Your collection is impressive Andrew and very well organised. Can you show me the Shakespeare stamp as well please?' he said passing it back to me and reaching for his notebook again.

I placed the pack into the two thousand and one editions and fingered through to April two thousand and eleven.

'Here we are,' I said not hiding a second bout of re-lief. 'The Fiftieth Anniversary of the Royal Shakespeare Company, King Lear.' I proudly pulled out the pack and showed him the contents once again. 'Not quite celebrating him,' I said correcting myself from earli-er in our conversation 'rather celebrating the modern Company that celebrate him.'

'Splendid!' he said, ignoring what he probably thought was my pedanticism. Making a note and finishing it with an exaggerated and expressive full stop, the inspector picked up his coat and bag, nodded in appreciation and strode purposefully to the door. He opened it and turned.

'Thank you once again Andrew and I'll keep in touch.' He opened the car door with the remote control.

I raised a hand to say goodbye and used it to gently close the door. I leaning against the inside of it with my shoulders when it shut and exhaled a long hard slow breath of anxious relief. I knew I had done nothing wrong but I hated it when people thought I may have.

22. Guilty by Association.
18th December 2022. (After)

I thought of Sassy's riposte to me about Clemmie. It had hit a nerve and I had taken exception to the remark. It was almost threatening and I couldn't let it lie. It had put me in mind of William Blake's poem 'A Poison tree'.

I was angry with my friend
I told my wrath my wrath did end
I was angry with my foe
I told it not my wrath did grow

I had to address this and quickly.

As it turned out I learnt quite a lot about myself through the auspices of others.

First Sassy; I caught up with her when I went to Hanbury to pick up Clemmie and take her out for a meal. She was still getting ready in her room and Sassy answered the door and let me in. I looked around for Ora but she was nowhere to be seen. 'She's out,' was the reply when I asked. I took the opportunity of asking her about the comment that had been praying on my mind for a while.

'Oh Andrew,' she said. 'I don't mind telling you and to be honest I'm glad you've asked because it shows you listened, you're interested and most importantly you've not been put off! The fact of the matter is that Lickey visited me a few months ago. She had discovered that I, like her, had shared a short liaison with Max Charles. We talked at length about him and I must say she was unsurprisingly quite vitriolic. We talked about his flawed character and his relationships with other people both men and women. Your name cropped up and we talked about your friendship and loyalty to him even in the face of the many challenges he presented. This was some time before the car accident. As a result we questioned whether your integrity was as reliable as the reputation you have established. I do not want to see Clemmie experience anything like I did. She is not as strong as me. That was the reason for the comment and I'm sorry if it came across as a veiled threat but if you did hurt her you would be dealing with me I promise.'

I was floored. I had never experienced anything like this in my life before. I had always valued my reputation as a man of integrity, honesty and character. All of these things were very important to me and it hurt to find these highly prized qualities questioned so transparently.

I gathered my thoughts and looked into her eyes earnestly. 'Sassy I don't feel I need to say this but I will. You must believe me when I say I have nothing but the most honourable intentions towards your sister and I care for her deeply. There is nothing that I would ever do to hurt her and whilst these are words, you may measure me by my actions so far and in the future.'

I must say I was smarting from the lashing I had just received. Especially since I had supported Sassy through the break up and smoothed the way for Lamont to help her through the disassembly of that relationship.

Any further discussion was curtailed by a radiant Clemmie bouncing down the stairs to greet me. Her beauty that night shone through and over the conversation and blinded me to any pain I may have felt. She made me raise an effortless smile. Nevertheless, we left together with the word 'vitriolic' stuck in my mind.

Second Max; my allegiance to him was once again hitting the fan and whilst I prized loyalty I could not condone blind faith in myself. For a mature man I was having to face a lot of questions that I had over the years been careful to avoid by astute husbandry.

It also made me think about some words that my father had given to me years ago.

'Be careful who you mix with lad. You will be painted with their colours whatever the outcome.'

How right he had been.

23. Punch Drunk.
17th February 2022. (Before)

'What do you want Max?' questioned Lamont as he answered the door.

'Well I'm pretty sure I want to punch your lights out you interfering old sycophant.'

Lamont's shoulders and torso tensed in a fight or flight response. He was an imposing figure slightly elevated on the house threshold. 'Don't even go there Max. You're out of order coming here and door stepping me like this. Go away before you cause any more trouble.' Lamont put out two outstretched arms with palms uppermost to block any physical advance.

'You're the cause of the trouble you interfering mealy mouthed loser.'

Max stepped forward aggressively and Lamont had had enough. He formed a fist from his palms and unleashed a right hand onto Max's jaw that had been brewing for some time. Max reeled and fell backward off the step reaching for his chin in reflex. He rubbed it feverishly before standing up quickly, the anger obvious in his eyes now. He came again but Lamont was ready and this time curled a left fist to his forehead. Max staggered and fell again. This time he didn't stand up but sat there dazed for a moment.

Max shook his head. 'You're going to regret that,' he shouted. The red mist had fully descended and he ran forward looking to drive into Lamont with a rugby tackle that would have taken them both into the entrance hall but Lamont was ready for him. He stepped forward and aside deftly for a big man before swinging a tight left uppercut into Max's ribs that bent an already off balanced Max double. A quick second punch with a right fist quickly followed into his temple that sent him sprawling to the floor. Max lay there dazed and holding his side. He had not expected nor considered such an able adversary and lay spread across the doorway. Max had been born with a muscular physique and he relied on his arrogant air of entitlement to gain ascendancy in relationships and on the games field. Lamont's physical fitness training and natural physicality had been too much for Max's hubris to deal with. What appeared at the outset to be a narrow contest was lamentably one sided. Lamont grabbed him by the scruff of collar and lifted him up and out of the entrance.

'Now go away before I call the police!' he said releasing Max from his grip but not before he had been propelled away from the house. The door shut and Lamont walked to the window where he saw a defeated and subdued Max Charles retreat to his car nursing his face and holding his side. He opened the car door and sat behind the wheel where he stayed for a couple of minutes before driving off at speed.

'Thank God for that,' thought Lamont though his own anger. He was thankful that the distasteful scene on his front door was over. He was aware that he had said that he wanted to punch his lights out to Andrew but not here and not like that. 'But what do I do now?'

The answer he ultimately gave himself was nothing. Providing Max didn't involve the police or seek further confrontation he would leave well alone. He was worried about his neighbours; someone must have seen the piece of theatre just played out on their front door. Lamont reflected on the encounter. He remembered his youth and the challenges he faced at school and in his community. The boys back then didn't take kindly to a thrashing and Queensbury rules were not in play. Being beaten was a form of disrespect that sometimes led to retribution later. A fight sometimes led to threats and possibly a blade and you chose your battles very carefully in those days. It was not unusual for gangs to hospitalise individuals who were not submissive to them. He thought he had left all that behind. He would have to think carefully about his next move and what to do if he needed to.

Max's initial reaction fitted those of the classic bully. He licked his wounds and kept very quiet about his exchange, too embarrassed to share it. He had lost in a fair fight that he instigated but his brash confident front continued. Nevertheless, Lamont had seen him for what he was and Max knew it. The clear message had been sent; 'Don't mess with me or those that I care about'. He felt confident that Sassy would have no more trouble from him.

Lamont had his own reasons why he convinced himself that Sassy didn't need to know about the physical violence and he resolved to keep that part of the apparent resolution to her 'problem' a secret. His ideas for how this relationship with Sassy might develop had been protected. Whatever and regardless of the consequences, if Max ever came back with more threats of violence he vowed, he'd finish it for good.

24. Clandestinity.
20th February 2022. (Before)

The phone call in Chaddesley Corbett was entering a passionate phase.

'I'm confused about my feelings for you Max and also your feelings for me. I can't stop thinking about our brief encounter at the party last week and what it meant....'

'Stop there Lickey. You're thinking too much into this. I find you very attractive and I want you. There, I've said it, you're gorgeous; I fancy you like crazy and I'd love to come over right now so that I could show you. You're not alone in thinking about the other night all the time and I regret that we couldn't take it further then. Do you want to?'

'What?'

'Take it further?'

Lickey blushed instinctively; she could feel her pulse beat in her temple and the blood coursing through her veins. She raised her hand to her mouth as if to silence her feelings. She knew the answer already but she had never dared ask herself the question. Yes, she felt guilt as she still had some tender feelings for Bartholomew. They had shared an intimate relationship for just under two years and she was very fond of him. Just recently fondness is all it had become and she had missed the thrill and passion that they had once shared. He had shown himself to be a risk averse follower not a leader. Certainly not the alpha male that she thought he was when she met him. Bashful not bold; indecisive not brave. A kind loving man who she might need in ten years' time, not now. Perhaps their reticence to move in together was a sign.

On the other hand she had known Max from school age when he was an untouchable and unassailable senior and she an innocent and invisible junior. She had nurtured a crush on him from afar during those years and the yearning she felt was part captured conquest and part desire. She knew he could be conceited and arrogant; she knew he could be privileged and dismissive. She also knew she found him fascinating and extremely attractive and she wanted him.

'Yes I do,' she whispered seductively.

'Then let's not wait. Yours or mine?'

'Yes, I mean no; and yours.'

'Can you come over now without attracting adverse attention?'

'Yes'. She heard the first phrase but was completely blind to the latter part of the sentence.

'I'll be waiting.'

Lickey hastily threw some things she thought she might need into an overnight bag. Don't stop to think she mused. Just go. She had not been prepared for this but it was everything that she had subconsciously hoped for. She jumped into her car and sped off the driveway not caring about adverse attention.

>>>> <<<<

During the drive over she had time to think. What am I doing? Is this what I want? What about Bart? How do I feel about him? Thoughts were whirling in her head but she continued to let her emotions drive her forward. She found a parking space a few yards from the house, approached the small front step and tapped lightly on the door. Max opened it immediately. She stepped inside and he greeted her with a light kiss. She couldn't help noticing the swelling round his right eye and the bruise on his jaw but she didn't go there. He closed the door and swept her up in his arms.

185

25. Dark Deeds and Money with Menaces. 3rd June 2022. (Before)

Early summer had been kind. The days lengthened, clouds seldom appeared and the sun looked down as a bright smile that only faded with the horizon. Short sleeves and shorts had quickly become the norm, whilst short pinafore dresses and sandals filled the pavements and parks. Elise had taken the short stroll down into the town centre to meet Balwinder at one of the many coffee bars that helped to keep the high street vibrant. He lifted the large cappuccino to his lips and held onto the taste whilst he thought about what Elise had just told him.

'But how do you know that?'

'Well at the moment I'll keep my source secret but I'm telling you, Bartholomew is up to something. What else is he doing snooping around in a hoodie at his age and social status if he's not trying to hide his identity? I didn't believe it at first until I saw this.'

Elise produced a photograph on her phone.

'I don't think that's conclusive,' said Balwinder.

'I agree,' said Elise, 'I mean I can agree that it's not conclusive but do you agree that it looks like Bart?'

'Well probably but not definitely. Anyway, this furtive character was in Sangita's garden, late at night and not appearing to do good.'

'Did she report it?'

'Not yet because she feels like we should maybe address it first before getting the law involved.'

'What does she suggest? Fingernail extraction or maybe waterboarding. I'd be happy to do a bit of skin flaying if that's what require,' said Balwinder ironically but with a little too much enthusiasm unbefitting of his station.

'What I suggest,' said Elise paying no attention to Balwinder's supposed jocularity, 'is that we confront him collectively and put it to him that we think it's him and what the hell is he playing at.'

Balwinder strokes him beard and shook his head gently from side to side.

'I'm uncomfortable with this Elise. Why don't we hand it over to the authorities and let them deal with it?'

'Because he's one of us and he deserves a chance to explain himself.' retorted Elise. 'And because that's what Sangita wants us to do. She really wants to give him the benefit of any doubt. As you say, it may not be him and it gives him a chance to say so.'

※》—※

Bart was looking at some papers related to land acquisition that was relevant to both his work and to his Court Leet membership. He had to be careful not to wander into a conflict of interest. He picked his buzzing 'phone up from the coffee table in front of him. It was Elise.

I wonder what she wants he thought. He tapped the answer button and sat back on his chair.

'Hello Elise what can I do for you?'

'Hello Bart, how are you?', said Elise and without stopping for an answer she went on.

'Bart I was wondering if you could help me out? I have a problem that you could possibly help me with. There are sensitivities that I couldn't share over the phone and Sangita and Balwinder are involved. I know it sounds mysterious but you have the skills and knowledge to really help me sort it out. If I could pop round with Sangita and Balwinder it would extremely useful.'

You've got me intrigued Elise. Any clues as to what it's about?

'Not really. It needs a face to face with all of us there to clear this up Bart, so I'd rather leave the rest until we meet. Sorry to sound cryptic but all will come clear and I know you can help us.'

Although taken by surprise Bart was interested. What is it that I can be so helpful with he thought.

'OK Elise. When would you like to meet?'

'Early this evening if that's possible'.

'Urgent and pressing,' thought Bart still without any clue. He wanted to know more now.

'Right, seven tonight at my place. I'll have a glass of Malbec waiting for you all.'

'Thank you Bart that would be lovely. I'll let the others know.'

Elise ended the call and breathed a sigh of relief. Stage one complete.

'That was an improbable discussion,' thought Bart. He was flattered and gratified that he was worthy of consultation but intrigued by the lack of clarity. Shaking his head as if to remove an annoying infringement on his day he moved back onto what he considered to be a more pressing task. I'll think about that later he decided.

>>> <<<

Elise sat in the back seat of Balwinder's car.

'Remember innocent until proven guilty. No early conclusions or further suppositions until we have given him every opportunity to explain himself; and don't try to lead him into a particular story. It may still be a case of mistaken identity on our part. Let him tell us. I think we'll know if we smell a rat.'

'I hope it is mistaken identity but I don't think so,' thought Sangita. They sat silently from that point on in nervous anticipation.

Arriving as planned at seven o'clock, Bart greeted them all at the door with hugs and handshakes. Showing everyone through to the sitting room he poured everyone a glass of the Argentinian Malbec he had promised and settled himself down in his favourite chair.

Nursing her glass on her lap Elise broke the silence that had descended on the room. This was not a time for small talk.

'Well Bart, thank you for agreeing to see us all. I suppose you have been wondering how you can help us all and I think I will start by showing you a short clip taken from Sangita's security cameras and ask for your comments.' She played with her phone briefly and then passed it over to Bart who took it gently from her hand.

'Just press play,' she said looking for any reaction in his face. Nothing visibly admissible in the first few seconds but then did she detect a hint of surprise?

The others looked on with equal interest. Bart's expression was measured but with no overt tension or shock as the video played out. 'Oh dear,' he exclaimed as the intruder climbed the hedge from the golf course and furtively entered into garden and began behaving suspiciously. Looking back over his shoulder, the hooded figure in dark jeans first hid behind a fir tree then moved towards the house and looked through the windows. Bart shifted in his seat. The figure tried the garden door handle and found it locked and then stared upwards to the upper windows unwittingly looking straight into the security camera located on the wall next to Sangita's bedroom window.

If this wasn't Bart then he had a look alike, thought Sangita. Even his slightly stooped walking gait was revealing.

At this point there was a small but significant change in Bart's expression that did not lead to an admission of guilt. The video played out with the figure slouching next to a garden wall beside a tall plant almost appearing to hide from view.

'This goes on for a further fifteen minutes,' interjected Elise, 'after which time he carefully leaves the premises climbing a garden gate and exiting via the front entrance driveway and onto the pavement in the direction of the village. Bart withdrew his gaze, handed the phone back to Elise and looked around the room.

'Well this is clearly Sangita's garden late at night and this chap has clearly not been invited for supper. How do you think I can help you all?' he said casting his gaze around the room.

The group looked at each other waiting for someone else to take the lead. Elise assumed the mantle.

'Bart', a short pause, 'we all think it's you.'

The frame where you look up to the camera is very clear and the movements appear to be very you. I'm sorry to be so direct but we all feel the hoody and jeans don't disguise you. Why on earth would you be acting in this way?'

Bart held his gaze upon Elise and then broke into a broad laugh. 'I'm sorry to disappoint you all but that's not me. Why would I be rummaging around Sangita's garden in the middle of the night? No, never and I don't know whether to be offended or humoured that any of you would think it was me. You come to my house and confront and accuse me of dark deeds and malicious intentions. I am shocked and disappointed.' Bart was warming up to his defence. His face began to redden slightly.

Sangita cast a look of and surprise, doubt and relief at Elise.

Balwinder was not to be defeated and broke the moment of awkward silence.

'So where were you that evening Bart?'

'Am I being interviewed by the police here Balwinder?'

'If you think that is necessary it could be arranged. You are with friends here Bart. We are all in shock that this could be you. None of us want it to be you but we cannot deny the possibility. We were hoping you can help us find a way to stop us believing it was you. If you can't then we will have to hand this evidence over to the authorities and let them decide what to do with it.'

Bart's mouth dropped and his shoulders slumped. He stared into the glass panel of the wood burning stove. A small tear rolled down his left cheek and he lifted his head to speak again.

'It is me but it isn't what you think it is. I'm not trying to steal or burglar your home Sangita. It's more complicated than that and I think it's time I shared my distress at the situation that I find myself in. I don't expect sympathy and I do expect a degree of disappointment by you because I have let you all down.'

'Not the hardest nut in the world to crack,' thought Balwinder ruefully but glad of the admittance anyway.

The group moved uncomfortably in their seats. Although they had come prepared for Bart's admission they had all hoped for a denial and a suitable explanation. His open admission was a shock.

>>> <<<

Bartholomew Bramble unfolded his story to his small and expectant audience.

'It all started with an act of kindness. I had managed to get myself into a bit if a mess with a gambling debt that I thought I could manage. Overtime and despite my best efforts to repay it, the debt mounted. Although I had placed it on my credit card and tried various means including switching cards to free interest offers I had run out of road and my repayments didn't cover the interest payable. Those interest

195

offers actually added more to the capital repayment and actually made matters worse. By then, the debt had mounted to forty-eight thousand pounds. On an evening drinking with Max and in a moment of alcohol induced madness I shared my sorry tale with him. He consoled me and said that he would lend me the money on much more favourable terms that would allow me to get on top of it. I was so grateful.'

Bart held his glass of Argentinian Malbec and became aware of his grip tightening around it.

'At first it seemed an excellent arrangement. Max wanted cash exchanges which I was happy to make on a monthly basis and I was able to relax in the knowledge that I was getting on top of it. I had been stupid but I had realised my stupidity and started to put things right. I was aware that I had confided in a friend and that had put Max in a position of trust and me in a position of weakness. The relationship began to change. It started with a request, asking me to 'go and pick up an ounce of weed for me' he said. 'No problem, you just go here meet the guy and do the exchange.'

His willing audience exchanged glances of surprise that Bart could have interpreted as looks of disapproval but he was deep in thought and missed the exchange. After drawing a short breath he carried on.

'Then it became more serious and when it became cocaine I said no. It was then that he told me that if I didn't get it for him then he'd tell Lickey and other friends what I was really like, what I'd been doing and I'd have no friends at all. He started calling me a loser and became physically intimidating.'

He let his chin fall to his chest and Sangita reached out her arm to comfort him.

'I suppose I **am** a loser. I didn't put up much of a fight. Like today as soon as you put me under a little bit of pressure I buckled. I'm really not made out for that type of life and just kept making the wrong decisions. His intimidation of me worked. I agreed to the pick-up and went disguised so that no one would recognise me. The meeting point was in a quiet lay by just outside the golf club late, always late at night but on the second occasion two men turned up and said I owed them more money than I had and that there were back payments still due. One of the men had a pair of pliers and went to grab my hand. I've seen films where that scenario doesn't end well. I panicked and ran. My legs took me into the grounds of the club and out across the first fairway. I could hear shouts and footsteps behind me but I knew I could outrun them. They were big powerful guys and somewhat overweight. My legs took me onto the ninth hole and although I could still hear sounds they were becoming more distant. The I remembered Sangita's house bordered onto the club grounds and thought if I could reach there I could hide for a while until they lost interest. I reached the edge of the rough behind the tee and the rest you have on camera.'

Sangita let out a sigh of partial relief and surprise.

'I never intended to hurt anyone or steal anything. I was merely hiding. It's a mess really and I have only myself to blame. I'm scared of Max and of the men that he's involved with and I've been taken down a rabbit hole of my own making. I'm so sorry for everything and especially to you Sangita for all the stress and worry I've caused.'

The room fell into silence once gain. There was so much to compute for everyone. From potential thief to betting addict and drug gofer. It was a lot to take in. This time it was Sangita who broke the silence.

'Bart I believe you. I think it is so ridiculous it must be true. You couldn't make something like this up, bless you.'

She stood up, crossed the room and put her arms around his still slumped and dejected body. 'This must be the low point from which you rise now and we will help you.'

The others nodded in agreement. Bart's reveal had impacted on all three present and an unwritten pact had been entered into. The man was undoubtedly in need of help and they would do what they could to salvage something from the metaphorical wreckage.

26. The Laughing Policeman.
24th December 2022. (After)

It was Christmas Eve and I should have been putting the last-minute touches to my Christmas. Instead, I was sat in conversation with DI Chandler who was increasingly and surreptitiously bringing me into his confidence. I was deeply honoured for two reasons. One, I naively suggested to myself, was that he no longer saw me as a potential criminal and two he valued our discussions. I did not swagger too much on the second as I was a realist and recognised he viewed our conversations as a sounding board for his thoughts and his musings. I allowed him the space to think and reflect and I think he appreciated it. Nevertheless, I was happy to be involved as I had become to hugely respect and like the man.

The laughing policeman stamp he held carefully in his hand came from Greeting booklet stamp 'Smiles' published in the February of nineteen ninety.

'Someone is laughing at me now Andrew. They're saying catch me if you can,' said Inspector Chandler. 'He or she may think they're being clever but this could be an early sign of over confidence. It could be their smug complacency will ultimately be their undoing. Ultimately goading me will not serve their purpose. On the other hand it may have come from another source. I have to ask myself who knows about the stamps already found and why would a third party become involved.'

I rustled uncomfortably in my seat and found myself looking slightly coy while readily agreeing with him. To toy with the intelligence of this man was a big mistake. It had many of the same markers as the envelope sent to Max. An empty envelope with two different stamps; this time postmarked Worcester, eighteen hundred hours on the fifteenth of December two thousand and twenty-two.; one of a laughing policeman accompanied by a stamp of a laughing clown from the same series. It had plainly been sent to antagonise and the purpose had been successfully delivered.

'What I am yet to fathom Andrew is the real intent. Is it a further clue to the identity of the killer? Is it a case of misdirection? Is it a poor attempt at an ill-advised joke? One could presume that the two envelopes are related but as yet I cannot even rely on that assumption.'

I nodded gently. I had been able to confirm the status of the stamps for the Inspector once again but could not answer any of the questions he posed. They appeared to be linked and they appeared to carry a message. Finger print analysis had yielded no one other than postal workers. Was this a smug messenger toying with the law or of which I was a willing participant or a third party laughing at it? Either way I was not amused but I observed the Inspector keeping an open mind.

'At least I have something small to work with.' He went on, 'It may be nothing but who do we know that was visiting Worcester on the fifteenth of December and how can I deduce it?'

I let the room fall into silence. I knew his rhetoric had wanted that and could tell he was pleased with that one small lead to work on.

'It is what we don't see that is important Andrew. We are lead to believe our perception is conditional on what we see, hear and feel; which in turn is reliant upon our memory. Here lies the rub; since all are memories are unique, we all see the world slightly differently. We must get into the mind of this perpe-trator to understand this person.'

Once again DI Raymond Chandler was broaden-ing my thinking. I envied his understanding of human behaviour.

'This is not a random event. As with most murders I am convinced that this crime has been committed by someone Max Charles knew well. Can I ask you to gather your society together?'

27. The Park House.
21st January 2023. (After)

It was easy to satisfy the Inspectors request. I had already booked the Park House suite in town for our next meeting and had informed all as such. Furthermore I explained to DI Chandler that it was to be an open house and so his attendance could be construed as one of interest rather than investigation. 'An excellent cover' he had remarked when I told him. I had remarked once that I was surprised that he was not a chief inspector with his knowledge, wit and stoicism. His reply, as ever was hinged with realistic pragmatism.

'It is something I have thought on Andrew but the fact is, investigation needs to be conducted on the ground. It is the central joy, if that's the right word, of what I do. Being a Chief takes the person away from on the ground investigation to overarching management of perhaps multiple cases. It is not something I have ruled out but I think right now it is for the future. One must consider what I believe to be General Custer's words on the matter.

'The true reward of leadership is leadership itself and not just a bigger tent'

'Not his last words I trust' I replied.

'No, they were probably 'Where's the fucking cavalry!'

We had both shared a hearty laugh. I had not heard him swear before and whilst surprised I appreciated the informality. 'He is a laughing policeman after all,' I had mused to myself.

The date of the twenty first was a Tuesday and was an available date. It didn't give a long lead in time or indeed much time to advertise to others. We all used word of mouth rather than spending money on promotion. It was better that way since there was some collective value in the room that I was very aware of and we had a better chance of policing the event if only people we knew were present. There was still the issue of security. It had occurred to me at our original gathering that by pulling together collections that in themselves had an individual value there was an expectation of a high total value in the room. Then I was inviting with some limited restriction members of the public who I did not know. Ignoring the protection of these precious objects and artifacts was inconceivable. I mentioned this to the Inspector.

'Quite right Andrew. You may hire some security if you wish but I am happy to ask Simone and Anthony to assist in this respect. They have alert minds and keen eyes. It also makes our presence even more plausible without suspicion. I can accredit their hours if I need to although there may be interest enough to ensure their cooperation without remuneration. Leave it with me.'

I was grateful for his help and annoyed with myself for not dealing with this oversight. I had got carried away with my big idea and had forgotten the little devil in the detail. I should have drawn up a tick list of things to do. I was usually quite good at sweating the small stuff and sent a mental note to myself that if the society were to continue we needed to develop a committee and spread the responsibility. I had my arms wrapped too tightly around my baby and it was time to let it go, if only by a little bit.

The suite was set in circular tables full of collectables across the range; none for sale but all available to view. Stamps, of course, coins, high end handbags and cinema scripts, as well as art work, jewellery and a selection of vinyl records of both the long playing and single variety. I gave a moment to the Flame Red Midget convertible outside. I had parked it with permission by the entrance of the building. It was attracting admiring glances as people drifted in and I was pleased by that. The evening started slowly. For the first half an hour we talked amongst ourselves but gradually enthusiasts and their friends wandered in, either out of good manners or genuine interest. I caught sight of Inspector Chandler with his team not long after and scanned the room for a reaction. There was none. Those who had met him before appeared unsurprised and those that had not would not know who he or his associates were. Though I felt sure our guests would be sufficiently enlightened by the end of the evening on our detective friends. By the time they had arrived and settled in arrived the room was abuzz with chatter and deep discussion. It was noticeable how busy Lamont was. People loved talking about music and all manner of folk seemed to wrap themselves into particular eras I had noticed. Perhaps that was why old rockers, like old soldiers, never died they just faded away. Taking my eye and my concentration from my collection of Russian Imperial stamps that had caused a bit of a stir, I noticed the Inspector made a line towards Bart. Good luck with that one I thought and returned my attention to a band of people in a growing debate on the ethics of holding Russian memorabilia at this time.

'Good evening Mr Bramble, how are you?'

'Very well thank you Inspector, if a little surprised to see you here.' Bart replied holding out his hand. I didn't know you were interested in collecting.'

Chandler reached out and broke into a soft smile. 'Just a little bit sir but Andrew has stirred an unknown inkling and when he told me about it I thought I'd come along to see what all the fuss was about.'

'Do you know sir that is exactly how I got started last year. I went along and just to see what was going on and the evening hooked me. Why not share the pleasure of all my visits to Villa Park over the years and get my programme collection from the loft and out of moth balls I said to myself. I've got ten seasons worth of programmes that record my purgatory and pleasure for the people's game in equal measure at that and other football stadiums. As well as that I am a bit of a Philographist.'

Not a word that the erudite Inspector was familiar with.

'I have no idea what you mean Mr Bramble, you've got me there.'

'Signatures and autographs Inspector. I used to reach out with my programme and get any of the players I could to scrawl their names over it. Failing that I'd hang around the ground after the match and wait for the players to leave and then I got a second chance.'

'A misspent youth then Mr Bramble?' The inspector didn't have him down as a football fan but demographics were an ever-changing thing.

'Oh I would never admit to that sir. Even to you. Can't tell a lie you see'.

'Can't you Mr Bramble?' DI Chandler mulled silently. He thumbed through a January 2006 programme. 'Ever been to Worcester Bart?' he said suddenly.

Bart was taken aback. 'Of course it's just down the road.'

'Ever been during the last year?'

'Yes, a handful of times. It is our county town you know.'

'Ever go last month?'

'Probably, it was the Christmas season after all. I shopped for presents..

'Probably or definitely?'

'Yes I mean definitely. You've got me all flustered. I didn't know I was being questioned!'

Di Chandler sauntered away, 'Oh you're not Bart you're not. I'm just asking,' he said sardonically.

Bart followed his path and watched him return before he placed the open programme on the table.

'Sorry,' he said.' Were you in Worcester by any chance on the sixth?'

'Are you having a laugh Inspector?'

'No but someone thinks I am,' came the reply.

He thought he saw a glint of recognition in Bart's eye but he couldn't be sure. He was happy with his first provocation and felt certain that Bart would not keep that conversation to himself. He would scan the room for movement as the evening progressed.

The sisters had created an interested magnetism with their exclusive selection of handbags. Even he had recognised that there was money on the table. Gucci, Prada, Chanel, Hermes and Dior where all represented in one shade or other. He was worldly enough to know what certain ladies would like even if they or their partner couldn't afford it. There was no Mrs Chandler but if there was he expected that she'd be hovering with the same enthusiastic attraction. He had gathered from Elise that there were some old classics in the collection.

'A bit like the original owner', he pondered cheekily a little embarrassed to even share the thought with himself. He selected his next prey.

'Good evening Lickey.'

She smiled politely. 'Inspector, so nice to see you. Can I interest you in some beautiful jewellery?'

That sounds like you're trying to sell it to me Lickey.'

'Only metaphorically sir,' she replied.

'Lickey what do you know about stamps?'

'Not a lot Inspector. Only what Andrew has tried to tell me and unfortunately some of that goes in one ear and out the other. My jewellery is my passion and I could tell you a lot about these pieces here but not much about stamp design or their provenance.'

Chandler nodded and lifted a fine eighteen carat gold bracelet with dangling charms. He studied them attentively and moving them around his left hand with his right index finger he swiftly changed the subject.

'You studied medicine for a while I understand?'

Lickey looked surprised. 'Well now Inspector that is correct. You do your research thoroughly.'

'That has been said to me before. Why did you give it up?'

'Too demanding Inspector. I found I was an intellectual lightweight after all and I'm not too prissy to admit it.'

Laying the bracelet down and stroking his chin he prodded further.

'You must have picked a few medical skills up along the way though?'

'Very little. I decided early on that the course wasn't for me and I persevered for longer than I should have for my father's sake. My heart wasn't in it.'

'What a shame. The profession needs caring people with a passion like you Lickey.'

'No shame Inspector. I'm happier now than I've ever been.'

'Oh and why is that?' he said probingly.

'Just life inspector, throwing good things my way. Enjoy the evening.'

Lickey had had enough of this game and began to tend to her display. She didn't know what he was after but she didn't like his tone. DI Chandler got the message and with a feigned salute and polite good evening he sauntered away with another grenade handed over. Three steps away he changed his mind. He turned scratching his head.

'Just one more thing Lickey. Why haven't you brought your stamp collection to share this evening.'

Lickey blanched visibly. 'She's going into shock,' he thought but before he needed to take any action she breathed deeply, regained some colour to her face and smiled.

'Oh Inspector it's far too small for anyone to take an interest in and besides it pales beside my jewellery.'

'Just the same I'd love to see it if you'd do me the honour.'

'Anytime Inspector. I'll give you a ring.'

'Thank you. I'll look forward to the call.' He wondered if he'd pushed too far only to discover he hadn't

'Maybe I'm barking up the wrong tree', he thought. A hypothesis was starting to form in the mind of DI Raymond Chandler, the cogs were all beginning to turn in a particular direction and that gave his mind a certain synchronicity too.

28. Point to Point.
28th August 2021. (Before)

Sassy had first met Max on a point-to-point race in Chaddesley Corbett. She was riding in a ladies intermediate race. He was watching and she fell off. He and was there to pick her up. That's how it all started, a struggling embrace in the middle of a muddy field. Soft ground as the racing fraternity say. He remembered her face had reddened under her riding hat and she appeared more embarrassed at falling off rather than his over strong manhandling as he helped lift her to her feet.

'Are you alright?'

'Of course,' she had said as she wiped the mud from her riding breeches. Bringing a forearm across her cheek she spread a splash of mud across her nose making it worse than it was before. Max was quick to pull his sleeve across his hand and wipe it clean for her.

'Under the circumstances that's a rather stupid answer,' he had replied.

She laughed and he reciprocated. He walked her over to her waiting horse and she re- mounted while he ignored the protestations and reprimands of the course marshals.

'See you at the finish!' she had shouted as she spurred Mulberry on with her heels and the horse responded immediately into a canter before finishing the race last. Sassy was unmoved and undiminished by the result. It was always fun to her.

Max and I had enjoyed the thrill of the course. We were close up to the horses as they jumped the fences and saw the skill of their riders as they manoeuvred the ground conditions. It was Max who had been keen to attend but neither of us knew much about its purpose other than a good day out and a few beers. It was Elise who had elaborated on the subject for me when I told her we were going.

'Oh you'll enjoy it Andrew. It is called point to point because the original riders back in the nineteenth century used to race from church steeple to church steeple. Of course nowadays it is a series of straight forward steeplechase races over fences around a course, designed primarily for amateur riders to maintain their skills during the close season for hunting'.

Elise knew how to enjoy herself and I picked up on her obvious delight by promising myself an experience.

The races were set against a back drop of open fields with Woodbury and Abberley Hills the protagonists on the horizon where Henry IV starved out a Welsh and French army in the fourteen hundreds. How we fail to learn from history I thought as I stared reflectively over those hills.

The course itself was set in a shallow, pretty rolling valley and the gradient that housed a gallery of cars had the appearance of a natural amphitheatre. It was an opportunity to enjoy splendid food and drink that spilled from well stocked raised car boots amid a myriad of portable chairs and foldable tables. The sun shone across the slope and we had wandered away from the crowd and taken up a position next to the rail at the fourth fence. We thought the start of the back strait was where we would feel close to the race. I was not sure we should have been allowed there but as it turned out it was an act of destiny.

I had never been involved in the equestrian fraternity and watching horses jump up close was a scintillating experience, leaving me in awe of both the rider and the horse. Before Sassy's fall it had crossed

217

my mind already that theirs was not a place for faint hearts.

I was at peace with Max that day. I remember it well. Having seen Sassy fall off and remount with so much gusto, the esteem in which I already held her had risen tenfold. 'She's either brave, stupid or a combination of both,' I had thought.

I had met the triplets before but it was the first time I had been drawn to Clemmie so keenly. Visually there were many similarities between the three girls. Ora was probably the most bubbly and restless of the women and demanded the most attention. She had blond hair -that was probably not her own but no one would dare ask- and blue eyes. A rounded nose and a small scar on her cheek from an old hockey injury gave her a unique attractiveness and instant recognition. I admired her for keeping that scar in these days of the obliteration of any perceived cosmetic blemishes. Clemmie was more thoughtful and reflective; she had a quiet and understated confidence that I liked. Slightly darker in complexion than her sisters with highlighted golden, brown hair and hazel eyes she had what my eye thought was an exquisite slender muscular frame than singled her out from the others. Sassy was the eldest and a height, composure and authority that naturally dominated the room. Some people are born to do that. Never has a name been more apt for a person. I guess that is what attracted Max.

We met up with the sisters at The Swan pub in the village afterwards and enjoyed a memorable hour with them before departure. We would have liked longer but we came a poor second behind the needs of Mulberry.

'Well congratulations to you Sassy. You are a formidable rider,' said Max as he placed the drinks on the large round wooden table. There were nods of agreement and looks of appreciation by the sisters and a satisfied smile appeared on Sassy's face.

'That may be true but how you arrive at that conclusion based upon what you saw today is questionable. You hardly saw me at my best,' replied Sassy.

'Oh I think I did. What resilience, fortitude and grit! What strength, determination and commitment! All there in abundance wrapped up in beauty.'

Sassy stared at him knowingly. 'Well what are you after Mr Charles?' she said flirtatiously.

'That's for me to know and for you to find out,' he replied.

The game had begun and a short silence followed. The sisters didn't know what to say until Clemmie intervened. 'She's a Cartwright Max. All of those things, all of the time. That's what Cartwright means in our house.'

I looked on in silent admiration.

Max was quick to follow up later that evening and contacted Sassy so that they could meet up again. I, on the other hand, was keen on Clemmie but had hesitated.

'There is only the quick and the dead Robert,' he had said laughing. 'The trail will go cold if you wait too long,' he added taking on the tone of a guiding father.

I could understand his attraction to women despite his lack of empathy. His confidence was off the scale and his Nordic looks and physical presence made female attraction seemingly easy for him. Some people, I decided, didn't need to try too hard.

Max fired up the Maserati in the car park. Awae were waved off as the sisters returned to care for their horse, Mulberry. It was early evening and he opened up the throttle on the motorway and the two of us drove around the foothills of the Malvern Hills and up to the car park closest to the British Camp. We stopped for a drink before heading back the twenty-three miles to home. He loved the exhilaration and excitement of the ride. I was not immune to the experience either. The roof was down and the wind ripped through and over our heads billowing our hair. I felt free and un-encumbered, well away from the cares of the world. I could see why he loved driving in that moment. Max carried many cares and disappointments, the majori-ty of which were of his own making. He had grown up with high expectations believing that he had a life where he would have everything. There had been a late teen awakening and a crashing reality that smashed into his adulthood, greatly surprising him. Needless to say he had not dealt with it particularly well.

Much later on and with the benefit of hindsight I had thought about the perpetual expectations that society continues to feed our children and the limitless world that we offer them from an early age. I think Max had suffered with a smothering of affection and opportunity, although doting on your children is not a crime. I thought how he used to get the very best of everything and was a little too proud to show off even from an early age. It ill-prepared him for the realities of life. The lovely people Max's parents were, and still are, they were probably lax in carefully nurturing him and providing him with balance. It was hard for me to be too critical as I had probably been too keen to foster

221

Max's excesses as well. My parents had provided a different reality and my father's guidance and supportive words provided at the appropriate time, rather than Max's glib phrases, had stood me in good stead.

'Happiness is not *the* target Andrew,' my father had told me. 'Contentment and satisfaction are. They are very different. Happiness is elusive and external and often dependent on others. The latter two are achievable and through internal experience. Chasing the first makes it run faster and further away but be kind to yourself and the world and contentment and satisfaction will find you. Be honest upright and have integrity at all times. No one has the right to expect all and everything.'

It may not have been these exact words but his sermon had been pretty close to it. My father had given me much but I would have been happy with a fraction of his profound wisdom.

I never questioned Max's motives with Sassy. Why should I? It wasn't my place and Sassy was a grown woman. Even knowing him for the time I did I never saw him as a user of people in that way. Yes, he liked women but that is only like many men. What I came to understand was that he had a selfish gratification that let him down when it came to any form of relationship. He had not been secretive with me about his clandestine trysts with Sassy but was more discerning in public thank goodness. There must have been something deep inside that knew he couldn't go public with his very private affairs. That, or he knew that it was in his own best interests. Perhaps I am too generous and it was really more of the latter. I am sure she would have been horrified if she knew I was aware of their affair and how it ended. I am sure her sisters were non-the-wiser of the infatuation that he held for their sibling. Whatever, the ending was not tidy and left an unpleasant taste. If Sassy wasn't the strong woman that I knew her to be I think she would have felt used and discarded. She was well within her rights to publicly denunciate him which to her credit she did not. She probably blamed herself; she was that type of woman and for better or worse would have relied on the resilience she had learnt from a young age.

I remember the still powerful lowering sun whilst we drove north towards home, carefree and light on worry that day. We both had a healthy glow by the end of it. Our sunglasses had protected our eyes form the buffeting breeze and beaten back the rays but our resulting contrasting panda eyes were a testament to the strong elements. They had raised a round of robust laughter between us as Max dropped me off in the fading light.

29. Another Dalliance.
21ˢᵗ January 2022. (Before)

Lamont was listening to the old classic 1972 album 'Talking Book' by Stevie Wonder. He had reached the last track on the album; 'You and I' was playing.

'In my mind we can conquer the world,' sang Stevie. 'In love you and I, you and I, you and I.'

He was supposed to be preparing his classes for the week and harnessing the best music for the activity but instead of going to Spotify he had begun fingering though his album collection. It helped his growing reputation for creative work outs and he enjoyed doing it. Initially focusing on the first track of the album 'Superstition' with its regular rhythm, tempo and dance leaning, Lamont had been drawn into listening to the rest of the album, allowing himself to be side tracked. Poor discipline on his part he thought but enjoyable just the same. He loved being self-employed in these moments. The freedom to choose; to indulge himself and not worry. He sat back in his chair, rested his elbows on the arm rests and made a bridge with his fingers. He contemplated the on-going lyrics and suddenly thought of 'Foxy Lady' by Jimmy Hendrick. He rummaged through his vinyl collection to find the Jimmy Hendricks Experience album 'Are You Experienced.'

'Here I come baby I'm coming to get ya, Foxy Lady.'

The big man was feeling romantic. He thought of Sassy. Now there was a woman. Feisty yes but confident, attractive, outgoing and fun to be with. He got the feeling she like him but how much? She certainly flirted with him but any more than she did with others? and to what extent should he mix business with pleasure. He didn't want to damage his business reputation that he had worked hard to build up by making a wrong move. Max had drawn her into his orbit and Lamont had heard on the grapevine they had had at least one date which could present a big problem. Was his attraction genuine or one of rivalry and contest. It would be bad timing to make a move under such circumstances and would not reflect well on his character. He was certainly attracted towards her but Sassy had an air which probably made most men feel the same. Perhaps he should not entertain such thoughts in the current climate but she had promoted a latent feeling in him. One thing was for sure, he wasn't going to let the egregious behaviours of Max Charles influence how he felt and there was no harm in letting his natural charms help her create a suitable distance from the train wreck that was his long-standing nemesis. He would be happy to pick up the pieces and help her recover.

'Just continue to be friendly and open and see where it leads. I have to be cautious with this,' he pondered.

Whatever he felt, Lamont knew that a head on play on Sassy, whether reciprocated or not, was likely to get contested physically and who knew where that would end? Both he and Max were big and strong and there would be damage on both sides if circumstances erupted. He knew that was not the way but he had to be ready for the heat. No, he needed another strategy and he was motivated.

30. A Conspiracy of Dunces.
13th November 2022 (Before)

They all agreed they had been slow to act. Their meeting with Bart was way back in June and although they had try to counsel him on how to deal with Max the situation had been increasingly difficult with continuing extortion and drug dealing. They had committed to help Bart but their help was not working. There had been a lot of talking but no action. What else could they do? Against all their moral scruples they had concocted a plan to confront Max and to conduct a friendly citizen's arrest and hold him until he saw sense and free Bart from his servitude and agree a financial settlement that they would all support. In their view they held the moral high ground and whilst they all worried about their plan they were convinced of it merit. They were driven by a conviction in the right of their action rather the possible consequences of it. Afterwards they had talked at length about how their actions jeopardised so much and how all their years of life experience and wisdom had deserted them, not just in a moment but for a significant while. Only fate of circumstance had saved them all and a silent pact had entered all their lives forever.

Balwinder was vocally dubious and thought the plan was like a script from a silent movie with a high level of jeopardy. He wondered afterwards how he had got himself into this mess and more to the point how he could get out. Nevertheless, he agreed to keep Max entertained. He would then have nothing further to do with it, he had decided and was forceful in telling this to the others. His view was that they should accompany Bart to the police station, where he could tell the whole story and engage the support of the authorities.

Elise said that this would implicate Bart in criminal activity, which was true but the consequences of this would be unacceptable; and get Max into big trouble and possibly a custodial sentence which they considered unnecessary. There was a better way she thought. Sangita agreed with Elise as she always did. Balwinder said they were not thinking straight and against his better judgement agreed to play host to Max for a few hours. He was adamant that he was washing his hands of anything they might construct afterwards.

The two women drew up their plan. Sangita would drive to his house and meet Max on his return. She would offer him a drink from her hip flask feigning to drink it herself first before passing him a draught of prepared dissolved rohypnol and whisky- something that Max would be unlikely to refuse and within fifteen minute he would pass out and Sangita would help him into her car. She would phone Elise who would prepare the ground for their arrival after contact was made and he would be taken to her house and placed in the cellar. He would be made comfortable but remain there until he was prepared to release Bartholomew from his debt (or at least help him manage it down) and accept he needed treatment for his drug use.

It was a half-baked and poorly executed plan which fortunately turned out to be its strength, thank goodness.

Balwinder had made me a party to their secret when he had confided in me after our cryptic meeting in the museum. It was something that I intended to leave locked up forever.

Sangita had parked her car away from street lighting in the village and had sat in wait with a good view of the house, flask in hand. She had not paid attention to the other cars on the street which later on she regretted.

Knowing the plan expected Max to arrive at approximately a quarter to eleven she had waited, becoming increasingly impatient and anxious so that by eleven o clock she started hyper ventilating and lost her composure and her nerve. She turned on the engine and hurried back home as fast as she could safely drive.

She drove past another parked car close to Max' house with a driver inside on the other side of the road. Both drivers were too involved with their own concerns to notice each other. She continued to drive through mono googles all the way home failing to register a green Morgan convertible deep amongst the bushes and trees on the other side of the road as she sped along the Kidderminster Road and back home toward Bromsgrove. She parked in her secluded driveway, crept into her house and up the stairs and carefully undressed. She slid into bed beside her sedated husband, wrapping her arms around him and fell asleep in the security of his presence.

31. More than a Collection.
6th November 2022. (Before)

The Norton Collection Museum is based on the Birmingham Road tucked between a doctors practice on one side and the flats and shops of the Strand on the other. Probably the most noted collector in Bromsgrove, Dennis Norton started collecting artefacts in 1949 and now the old coach house building is packed with information and objects that throw an illuminating light into the history of the town. It is a four-minute walk from my offices and I had spent many a happy lunch hour browsing through documented time and space in its hold.

The museum serves to illuminate and inform us all of our Bromsgrove heritage. Buckingham Palace Gates, the Canada Gates in Green Park and Liverpool's Liver Birds all found their origin in the town. It brings to mind the members of the Bromsgrove Guild who designed and built all of them – artists of their time from the arts and craft movement and an organisation that outlasted many of the other movements of that period. It also reminded visitors of the nailing cottage industry which found its origin in the seventeenth century and flourished in the eighteenth and nineteenth century because of the availability of coal and iron in the area. Some of those cottages can still be seen around the town and make small yet comfortable homes for families today. They are a far cry from the filthy rented little brick shops where men, women and children ploughed their trade. The preservation of many of these memories is down to Dennis Norton.

I was there to meet with Balwinder who enjoyed local history as much as me and had been stirred to start his own collection of Indian Artefacts from the Punjab as a result. He had some fine examples of Phulkari flower embroidery; a miniature portrait of an old Maharajah and beautiful old Punjabi dolls festooned his home. It was proving an expensive hobby and he had found websites were the most cost-effective way of trading up his collection. Despite his recent enthusiasm for collecting film scripts he was most at ease talking about his map and chart collection though. Like all of us he was a social historian. He collected what he liked but took great pleasure in finding out more. It was the intellectual curiosity and thirst for knowledge that drove him. This interest in life and how we arrive at where we are always made our conversations interesting. Today's chat proved more cryptic however.

I met him inside browsing over a parade of old shop fronts one of which housed a collection of old radios or wirelesses to be precise. From what I could see from a short distance away he looked full of care and carried a furrowed brow.

'Hello Bally. Not like going on the net today is it?' I said pointing at the window display.

He smiled a half smile. It was obvious there was something he wanted to tell me.

'Good afternoon Andrew.' He shaped his mouth to speak but stopped as if contemplating his words carefully. When he next deigned to speak he got straight to the point. 'Thank you for coming.' Another pause then, 'I want to tell you a hypothetical story of some people I know In India and tell me what you think of their actions.'

I was intrigued. No formalities this afternoon. 'Alright. Tell me more,' I said.

'In a local rural village there was a man who had broken the law and instead of calling the police a group of people in the village decided to take their own action against him.'

More silence that I eventually broke.

'Um, probably not wise but go on.'

'They decided to frighten him and took him to a cellar where they interrogated him about his actions and tried to blackmail him into a promise that he would not repeat his behaviour ever again. They said that if he did make that promise they would release him and not tell the police of his crime.'

He licked his lips as if to wipe away an unpleasant taste and I filled the on-going vacuum he kept creating.

'So they conducted an arrest without warrant, in other words, a citizen's arrest which does have some merit if they were sure he had broken the law. Even so and as you will already know, here in the UK there are strong guidelines for this. Then they kidnapped him and made him their captive. The first bit of potential good is overshadowed by the consequent bad. They should have handed him to the police as soon as possible and practical. They have followed this up with blackmail and menaces. It doesn't look good if they get found out.'

'I thought so too Andrew. That's why I wanted to ask your legal opinion. I will contact my friend and advise him appropriately although I fear it is already too late.'

'Just remember that our legal jurisdiction doesn't cover India my friend,' I added just covering myself. Regardless, there was a sense of relief in his body language as if he had purged himself through the conversation. With that came an abrupt change of subject.

'Let's go and have a look at those old motor cycles shall we?' he said.

I agreed but remained a little bemused by the story. It was most unlike the very mindful and relaxed demeanour I was used to with him but we were successfully diverted by the nineteen twenty, made in Bromsgrove 'Banshee' motor bike on display. We admired the workmanship together but later the story kept repeating in my mind like a piece of music on loop.

32. An Enlightening Visit.
24th January 2023 (After)

It was a grey and wet day that for many would simultaneously obscure the view and dampen the mood. Not that Raymond Chandler would let climatic narratives affect his waking hours. He was too busy and too pre-occupied to worry about weather conditions. He had the lead he wanted and he was going to follow it through thoroughly. He knocked on the door with his brown gloved knuckles.

Lickey opened the door. 'Come in Inspector.'

She had dressed for her important visitor in a midi length skirt and a white Arron tight fitting crew neck jumper. Her blonde hair was brushed back over her shoulders and Chandler noticed that his opinion she had put on a little too much make up for the occasion. He could see why men may be attracted to her.

'I've put out my stamps for you to view as you asked. I had no idea that you were interested in such a small collection.' She pouted and moved silkily from her doorway into her sitting room where the stamps had been laid out carefully. He could not help notice her flirtatious behaviour. He noticed the stamps had been removed from a purposely sized box and laid out on her coffee table. He took the liberty of taking a seat next to the collection.

Raymond Chandler had decided to be direct and to the point. There was nothing to gain by beating about the bush.

'Thank you Lickey. I very much appreciate your willingness to help. I have to admit that wanting to view these stamps has more to do with the case rather than a genuine interest in stamps'. He kept his eyes on her as he shifted in his seat to get a better position to browse.

The only observable facial response was a slight look of disappointment. 'Surely she realised that my only interest was professional,' he postulated.

'Well my collection is purely based upon presentation packs, all pre-ordered and delivered during the period nineteen ninety-two to two thousand and twelve Inspector. A teacher I admired at the time told me they were interesting to collect but I don't think it was good financial advice now and I was slow to stop the direct debit order from the royal mail. Some of them didn't even arrive through the post and so there are a few missing. I haven't really taken much notice over the years.'

'That's convenient,' he thought, 'and rather well-rehearsed too.'

She went on. 'Some of them are quite pretty and others informative but I seldom look through them now. I have thought about getting rid of them altogether but have never got round to it as yet.'

Chandler did not reply but took out a pair of delicate white cotton gloves from his Barber jacket chest pocket and exchanged them for his rather damp brown leather gloves which he placed on the chair arm before handling the envelopes carefully. He leafed through to 1999. There was the 'Smiles' pack in full including the laughing policeman. He smiled ruefully back at it. He fingered through to the two thousand and one navy set. This was missing in completion and no sign of a skull and cross bones. He felt a slight increase of the pulse in his temple. Now for the two thousand and eleven Shakespeare set. Taking his time to work through the collection he reached the year and slowing down, stroked through each edition. He leafed each set in their turn, passed where he thought it would be and finished inspecting the year. He retraced, worked through from December to January. No sign of the celebration of the Royal Shakespeare Company nor of the stamp inscribed with the words *'Who is it that can tell me who I am?'* He felt the hairs on his neck rise.

'Lickey, is there any chance you may have not quite collected in date order or inadvertently misassembled?'

She leant forward and looked up at him from the top of her lids submissively and provocatively. He was in no doubt she was trying to misdirect and steal his concentration, like a Siren leading boat worthy mariners onto the rocks. He had faced this before and he knew how to remain aloof.

'Unlikely Inspector I just added the next one to the front of the box as it came through the post. When I have got them out to look at I usually leave them in the box and flick through them. As I said, some of them failed to arrive but I couldn't tell you which.'

That fail safe get out of jail free line again.

'Can you give me ten minutes to examine them more closely please? You don't need to be here if you don't want. Please feel free to get on with whatever you need to.'

He thought he saw a slight startle in her eyes – a raising of the eye lids; a pursing of the lips -not this time a provocation but a reaction -or was it his imagination?

'That's OK. I'm not pressed for time and I knew you were coming so have no other plans.'

In his meticulous way he gathered up each year in turn and carefully eyed each pack before checking their date order and putting them aside. The room fell silent. He estimated he had probably rifled through two hundred and fifty envelopes in just over half an hour. It was well worth the time. There was no sign of either of the incriminating stamps.

He placed all stamps back in the box in date order, placed the lid decidedly on the top and sat back in his chair.

Lickey sat forward in anticipation, elbows on her knees, her hands supporting her slender chin.

'Ms Farrier, we need to talk honestly and candidly. I am going to ask you about two specific stamps that were sent on an envelope to Maximillian Charles by hand prior to his death. Did you send that envelope?'

He was more astute than she anticipated and it winded her. Lickey thought carefully about her response and there was a strong hint of preparedness in her next sentence. It surprised him.

'Yes I did Inspector and I'll tell you why.'

Chandler sat back in his chair. He was startled by her words, fully expecting a denial, especially since she had carefully prepared the ground in her assertion that not all of the packs had arrived.

He quickly decided that that would have been too much of a coincidence.

'She's a clever cookie,' he mused. 'She's decided to double bluff me.' DI Chandler wondered how he would unravel the truth and whether he was as good as he thought he was.

Lickey spent the next hour outlining her relationship with Bartholomew, her affair with Max and her treatment by his hands; his verbal abuse of her and her family; his belittlement, his coercive control and her biggest regret of all – how it had affected her relationship with Bart. She explained to DI Chandler that the stamps were meant to threaten and intimidate him into leaving her alone; that was all. She thought it was a clever thing to do at the time and she had taken care that she could not be identified as the sender. She had realised later that Max would not understand or appreciate the subtlety; he was too full of himself for that. She had regretted it soon after but didn't want to own up to it after Max's death as she realised that it may implicate her and cause suspicion which of course it now has. She was innocent and naïve and although not saddened by his death she was not the cause of it. The detective sat motionless throughout and listened intently to all she had to say.

33. Back at the Office.
24th January 2023 (After)

Black and Jackson were staring at their respective computer screens when DI Chandler came in. He paced across the room full of intent, stroking his long front locks back and licking his lips.

'The mood board if you please', he said pointing to the wall. They coalesced willingly.

He explained to them that it had been Balwinder who had broken the pact. He had been unhappy for a long time about the wall of silence regarding Max Charles's drug abuse in an attempt to protect Bart from being identified as a supplier. He had gone along with something that he knew to be wrong and it was eating at his conscience. The wall came tumbling down when he was confronted with a fact that he could not deny. Yes he did know and he knew that Bart was acting as his gofer. DI Chandler found it hard to hide his satisfaction but he was unaware that he was not being told the full story. Balwinder had only shared a paragraph of what he knew. Nevertheless, Chandler was pleased that he had been able to break down another little wall but waited until he was back at the office to share his pleasure. He had a broad beam of a smile across his face. He began to unravel his stream of consciousness before they had left their desks.

'The roads are converging, my dear people, and they appear to be arriving with Lickey Farrier standing at the junction. The problem we have now is that there is a confident and continued denial against increasing evidence on her part. We need to pin her down with corroborated fact and cross-referenced material. We can't attach her physically to the scene yet but we have the following: -

One. Motive: take any combination of fear, betrayal and revenge. Jilted lover of the victim; admits to being coercively controlled; involvement with MC caused break up of another relationship.

Two. Credulous evidence: admits to sending threatening messages via symbolic stamps and the hair found in the victim's car is shown to be hers through DNA. I grant you, not necessarily related to the night in question though she admits to being in the car on more than one occasion.

Three. Weak Alibi: Late night telephone call to her home does not mean that she was there all evening and she has no other alibi. She says she spent the evening watching TV. Get the schedules for that night and ask her forensically what she was doing throughout the evening, what was she watching and what was going on in those programmes at various times.

Four. A witness that incriminates Bartholomew Bramble in the supply of illegal Class one drugs to the victim. Our most vital asset and yet the witness incriminates himself that could lead to a sole conviction if we don't prove there was collusion.'

The hard-working assistants sensed the time for orders was coming and they weren't disappointed.

'I want you both to interview Bartholomew Bramble together. I need to know the context of his relationship with Max in the light of new evidence, why has he withheld vital information but also the content and context of the 'phone conversation with Lickey that night. Also take a look around his house and try to ascertain if he also collects stamps. I'm interested in the laughing policeman thread and really want to track that down. It doesn't make sense yet. Also, why did he 'phone Lickey when their relationship had faded because of Max Charles. We've missed the ebb and flow of that relationship so far and I need to catch up on it quickly. Pursue that line of questioning. We have the scent, now hunt it down. Do your work and I think we can bring Lickey in under caution. Meanwhile there's an itch I've got to scratch with Andrew Byron and we'll meet the day after tomorrow.'

With that he strode out of the office with the same intent as he came in but there was now an observable extra spring in his step.

34. An Economy of Truth.
26th January 2023 (After)

'I think I may have misjudged you Andrew. You convinced me of your candour yet I sense some recent holding back'. Di Chandler didn't hold back.

'How so Inspector?'

'When we last met you blushed when I asked who else possibly knew about the first stamps that were sent to Max. My instincts tell me you are protecting someone Andrew? May I remind you of the consequence of perjury or worse still an accessory to murder.'

The words stung me like an angry wasp that wouldn't let go. As I thought, this man missed nothing and would not countenance a breach of faith. I took a deep breath – he had a habit of making me do that and I prepared to unburden myself as what I had found out was suffocating me.

'I've been troubled by this since we last met and am sorry to say I have broken your confidence and confided with a loved one who I entrusted with certain information. This, I have learnt, was in turn passed to a third party and it seems was played out as a bad joke that all now regret. I was coming to tell you but as ever you are ahead of my game.'

DI Chandler frowned and pursed his lips. 'This is not a game Andrew but go on.'

I knew he meant me to talk in detail rather than accept a summary.

'Well, in a moment of bad judgement I did share the suspicious stamps element with Clemmie one night. I swore her to secrecy but I've have just recently found out she told Ora. It was she who thought it was an interesting twist and she found it enthralling. When there was no apparent progress in the investigation she had assumed, quite wrongly and without warrant, that the police were not doing enough. She bought the stamp on the internet and sent it to you. It was, as you rightly suggested back then, 'a poor attempt at an ill-advised joke'. No one could be sorrier than I and although I am disappointed with both Clemmie who I confided in and Ora for her shocking naivety, I blame myself for the initial indiscretion and breach of confidence.'

He stared at me and through his eyes I could almost see the cogs of his brain working to formulate the most appropriate words for someone whom he had trusted. I could feel disappointment seeping from his pores whilst I had to blink away the moister that was gathering in my eyes. I think that was invoked from the fear of his potential wrath.

'You do know that this is possibly a matter on which you have perjured yourself Andrew and I will have to think long and hard about a way forward from here. On the other hand, I also am not without fault as my investigative strategy is always risky.'

I nodded hanging my head in shame. Silence fell upon the room and although I was used to this in our conversations it was a quiet that felt more oppressive and threatening than I had ever known.

He continued.

'At best I have placed another piece of the jigsaw into the picture and closed down an area of investigation. At worst I have opened up an untruth that conspired to unwittingly mislead and waste both mine and my officers' time. Although I find it hard to forgive I recognise my own investigative frailty and methods. You must not discuss this matter before I have spoken to both Clemmie and Ora Cartwright. Do I have your word?

I was surprised he had asked for my confidence again after I had let him down so badly.

'Yes Inspector you do.' I felt sick with both worry and disappointment within myself. I still do to this day.

⋙ ⋘

DI Chandler did not hang about. Within twenty-four hours he had interviewed both Clemmie, Ora and myself who were all equally devastated by our foolishness. It was a cause of acute embarrassment and secret shame. Sassy was in shock. She couldn't believe her sisters could have been that foolish and her opinion of me once again took a nose dive.

The Inspector 'invited' me to another one of his 'meetings' late in the day.

'Listen carefully Andrew. I told you at the beginning of this investigation my methods were unconventional and not universally popular with those superior to me. I stand by my methods because in the main I have, if I may, gathered an outstanding record of investigation success. I am confident in that assertion.

254

This is, in part, a consequence of the decisions I make regarding who I trust and chose to share with. That is my risk and my risk alone. It is hard to blame you for sharing with both Miss Cartwrights when I have given you the bullets to fire. Nevertheless, I did not expect you to compromise that faith by firing the gun. Equally, Clemmie Cartwright acted as a rolling stone, gathering willing moss in the guise of her sister. In many ways I am glad that Ora's attention turned to me rather than the mossy stone gathering pace and reaching people further down the hill.'

He paused to draw breath and I felt like the punch was coming soon.

'So I have decided that I will not pursue any further any possible charges and you will not face prosecution. This applies to both you and Clemmie Cartwright. I have already spoken to Ora and have issued her a fixed penalty notice for wasting police time.'

Whilst I felt some responsibility for Ora's fate, the world which had lain upon my shoulders lifted and returned to its orbit. My legs groaned from the release of that weight and remained unsteady.

'As I have said I must bear some of the responsibility and I have reflected on that in reaching my decision.

You are all lucky people Andrew,' he explained. 'Were it not for my methods and the fact that I think I have more use from you as an informant and anthropologist then I may have gone down a different route. We are collectively culpable and that arm of this investigation can now be closed.'

I had yet another reason, amongst the many, to admire the man but I knew then why he had not climbed the career ladder as far as he should have. His risk-taking methodologies would not have been received favourably by those superior to him. They had probably taken a chain saw to his ambition in that respect.

35. The Arrest. 3rd March 2022. (After)

When Lickey was finally arrested under caution for questioning it was Bart who had willingly capitulated and disclosed the secret that had bound he and her closer together again. He could not stand the thought of her being interrogated and held in a cell and no longer believed in the longevity of their secret pact. Sitting alongside her solicitor Lickey had listened to the words:

'You do not have to say anything but it may harm your defence if you do not mention something when questioned that you later rely on in court. Anything you say may be given in evidence.'

Bart had sat at home and could see the writing on the wall and did not want her to suffer exclusively as a consequence of the actions of them both. Not only that but knew that if she did tell the full story she would implicate him anyway. He 'phoned the contact number he had been given when the investigation had started and willingly waving his rights to legal representation and attended an interview to give his own sorry story as well as Lickey's tale of woe. He did not hold back, giving a detailed account of all events leading up to and including the night of the murder.

DI Raymond Chandler smiled internally with satisfaction. It had been easier than he had anticipated. 'Eighty percent of the juice from twenty percent of the squeeze,' he had silently opined to himself.

Bartholomew Bramble had wanted Maximillian Charles dead for sure. He had dishonoured and defiled his girlfriend, using and leaving her without recognising that she still had feelings for him. Bart recognised her infidelity but had forgiven it. He loved her. She had run to him to say sorry and he had opened his arms to her once again. He had shared his story with her, the gambling addiction, the loss of financial stability, the seeming support of Max and then the expected payback. Together and full of revenge, they had both hatched a plan to be rid of him forever. It had nearly gone to design but for the car crash and from then her actions had become spontaneous. She had seen his car on the roadside and acted in malice and rage to ensure he did not survive. After injecting him she had smashed his head into the steering wheel and left him for dead. Bart's part had been played out at Balwinder Singh's house; coordinating the timing of departure and allowing Lickey to get into place. He had arranged for the delivery of the drugs from the same supplier that had been used for fulfilling Max his recreational habit. He had not delivered the arrow but he had pulled back the bow.. He was willing to sign a written confession.

Now for the final twenty percent of the squeeze, thought Chandler.

Lickey Farrier did not cooperate and lived up to her name by clipping away at the truth. She had bridled at the accusations and refused to be saddled with them. The policeman had been pleased with his metaphors and allowed himself a short inner chortle. He had to give Lickey her dues, she was convincing. Why would she kill someone following a short affair? It must have been Bart – he had the motive, had the means, obtained the drugs, planned the evening, knew the location.

There was incriminating yet only circumstantial evidence and no direct line linking her to the crime scene. Yes, she had been in the car at other times and it was not surprising that a hair of hers was found. Yes, she had sent him the threatening stamps out of frustration. Yes, she regretted and resented his advances. Yes, she had rekindled her relationship with Bart but no, she did not kill Maximillian Charles. She was convincing but the detective had heard these types of denials before. In effect she was throwing Bart under the bus.

DI Chandler needed to squeeze harder and surprisingly he wanted me to supply the pressing.

'We must break this shield Andrew. We could give this to the Crown Prosecution Service, go to court with what we have and let the jury decide but I want this case wrapped up and put to bed within twenty-four hours, otherwise I'll have to apply for another forty-eight hours under exceptional circumstances. All the evidence points to her but she is in a state of denial and needs good advice from someone she trusts.'

She had agreed to meet me in an empty room, save for two utilitarian metal and wood chairs and an old worn wooden desk where we sat facing each other. There were no police or a solicitor, no paper or pens, no recording paraphernalia; just me and her. She'd been crying, her hair was ragged and she looked tired. A far distance from her days of innocent elegant simplicity.

I couldn't help but feel sorry for her. I guess I looked tired too. I was certainly feeling it. We stared at each other across the small divide.

'How are you?'

As good as I look,' came the reply.

'Is there anything I can get you?'

'A taxi home would be good.'

I looked down, playing with my fingers.

'How's Bart?' she asked.

'I don't really know. Just that he's been arrested and charged.'

Her face saddened. 'I didn't do it you know.'

I left a space. I had come to know the power of the noise of silence.

'Lickey?' A shuffled pause and a pretext for more.

'You realise Max was my friend and for that I feel responsible? You are my friend too and I feel the weight of that. I don't want you to suffer any more than you have to. There are only two real possibilities remaining. One, Bart acted alone or two, you acted together. If the truth is you acted together and Bart pays the price you may have to live in that knowledge for the rest of your life. There is only one ultimate truth and the sharing of that truth releases you from fear, allowing you peace.' I was thankful for those self-help books I had read over the years. 'Imagine living with the knowledge of subterfuge for the rest of your life. You can no longer be the authentic you ever again.' I thought I had dressed this whole catastrophe up well but she was not for turning.

'Who am I Andrew? Do you really know me? Do you know my life, my existence? Yes you are a friend but there are limits to any friendship or to that confidence. You were a friend to a man I could not trust, who wanted to use me and cast me aside. Why should I trust you?'

She had a point. It made me wonder what I was doing here.

'You're right Lickey; but right now I'm the best you've got. I suppose you've got to weigh up if you can live with your version of the truth going forward and whether you can rewrite yourself into a new narrative that remoulds who you've been and what you've done'.

'So you don't believe me Andrew? Then how can you be my friend?'

Another touché.

'Sometimes the best friends are the ones that challenge Lickey, not the ones with blind faith.'

262

Again I caught the heavy irony of what I had just said and wondered what the real purpose of this encounter was for.

She lifted her head and looked into my eyes.

'What do you see?' I asked and got back something that I wasn't expecting from her. '

A soft caring soul. An intelligence and a calmness. Something and someone who I could have done with years ago.'

I blushed. I had been doing that a lot recently and it was exposing me.

She smiled, I guessed for the first time in a while.

'I know why you're really here Andrew. You've been sent to make me see sense. To encourage me to own up and take my punishment. You might as well go.'

I stood slowly and walked towards the door. It wasn't just Lickey who had had enough. There were some uncomfortable truths that I had to face. I turned and looked pleadingly at her.

'Tell Bart I love him and we'll do this together,' she said. 'He wouldn't survive another rejection and betrayal from me anyway. Now tell the Inspector that I'm ready to see him.'

She had at last recognised that there was no other way out for her or for him.

DI Chandler was feeling confident as he entered the room accompanied by Simone Jackson but he knew there could still work to do as he had been this close before only to be disappointed. Lickey appeared more relaxed than he was used to and he thought perhaps she had already begun to ease her burden. Maybe the twenty percent squeeze was going to be more like a gentle coax.

'You have asked to see me Lickey?'

'Yes Inspector. I have no need of representation and waive my right to a solicitor. You will only need to listen. You'd better have your recording devices switched on and your pen at the ready.'

So it began with few pauses and little emotion. A flood of catharsis and self-justification without any visible remorse.

Lickey, apparently acting alone, had lain in wait outside the Chaddesley Corbett house under cover of darkness and had planned to put a syringe full of cocaine in Max's neck. She had done her research and entered into his dirty world of illicit drugs to get what she needed. She had not acted completely alone since Bart had helped her in this and he had been aware of her intentions and supported her motives. The cocaine would be mixed with fentanyl – a substance more than fifty times more potent than morphine she had learnt. If the opioid didn't stop the breathing on its own the overdose would kill him. She had decided. He had ruined her life, treated her with contemptuous distain and attempted to spoil a loving relationship that she had taken for granted. Yes, some of that was her fault but he was to blame the most. She hated him and that hatred had grown with each passing day. He had violated her and then rejected her and this was going to be her revenge. Now she was going to cauterise the wound she had suffered. She knew Max was drinking with Bart at Balwinder's house and would wait under cover of darkness and pounce on the bastard as he arrived home and put the key in the door. She was a woman possessed. Her eyes burnt with loathing and there was no going back. She failed to notice Sangita's car on the opposite side of the road light up and accelerate away about eleven o clock. She sat there for another hour. 'This is not right,' she had thought and without thinking things through she resolved to go straight to Balwinder's house without a plan for what she would do when she actually got there.

The plan altered again since Max smashed the car and almost killed himself anyway. A job well done Lickey had thought later, it had made her job easier. Had he still been at Balwinder's house the whole plan would have been jeopardised and for better or worse she would have been living a different reality.

Navigating the windy road she had noticed what appeared to be a foggy bend but as she drew closer she realised it was smoke drifting away from the road side. She slowed to a stop. Peering through the window she saw the car. She knew it. Winding the window down for a better look she peered into the gloom. It was green and she recognised the tail plate. Drawing her car close to the verge but not on it, she got out and crossed the road. Breathing heavily she found Max trapped and unconscious but still breathing. What a stroke of luck she had thought amidst the carnage. Taking a deep breath and without further pause for thought she went back to her car looking up and down the road for other vehicles. There were none. 'Shall I chance it?' she had thought. Quickly she went into her bag and took out the prepared cocaine and fentanyl mix. Rushing across the road she plunged the syringe into his neck. She knew Max would have experienced breathing difficulties and high blood pressure but with his injuries as a result of the collision there would be no coming back. She was confident that he would fade quickly into oblivion as a result of catastrophic organ failure. Death was certain and it had exhilarated her. She looked at the unconscious forlorn face. Reaching in through the broken window and across the passenger seat, she grabbed his hair and slammed his face into the steering wheel in a moment of vicious and victorious euphoria.

Composing herself she checked she had touched nothing. She was running on adrenalin now. Her footprints, what about her footprints? She scoured the area quickly for decent branches looking nervously up and down the road. Each second that passed increased the chance of a passing car. Grabbing a sturdy branch she had chopped up the mud where her shoes had left marks and dragged it backwards as she went to the roadside. The events had intoxicated her. She took off her shoes and ran bare foot across the road. She had dreamt of this moment and it was better than she had imagined. Throwing her shoes through her open window, she got back into the car parked alongside a still deserted road and accelerated away. She had driven home, planning how to dispense with the syringe where it would not be found. The adrenalin coursed through her veins and she remembered breathing heavily. She drove the car straight into the garage with its electric up and over door and waited in the driving seat until the garage door had shut fully. She had gathered up the dirty trainers and stepped into the house through the integral door into the laundry area. She paused and leant back against the wall, feeling the pulse in her neck still beating fast. She recalled the moment of sweet revenge thinking the gods had been with her that night.

The phone had rung as she sloped against the wall. She closed the door quietly and listened to the silence for a second. 'It's over, ' she had breathed quietly yet clearly and had pushed the button to end the call. Bart had said nothing in reply as they had planned.

She closed down her phone, stepped back into the garage and stripped off the pair of dirty black jeans, the black peaked cap and the old black jacket and stuffed them into a black bin liner. She squeezed the bag into an old holdall and zipped it securely. The following day she had started a small bonfire in her garden. She couldn't be exact but a few days later she had entered the Lickey Hills Country Park, in the cover of night. She had quickly found a secluded corner and poured out the ash remains of the burnt- out clothes from the same bin liner and holdall. She had wrapped the syringe in newspaper and then dispensed with the bags and syringe amongst other waste at the nearest household waste centre.

DI Chandler had hardly dare to move. The unravelling had been quick and thorough and had been driven like an express train through all reasonable doubt. He had listened attentively to the circumstances as they developed and could not help feeling some empathy towards Lickey Farrier. She had been wronged but did wrong in return. She had been the victim of some coercive control but this had sent her over the edge. Murder was murder after all and there was no going back once committed. He switched off the recording.

'Thank you Miss Farrier', he had said. ' At this stage I would strongly recommend legal representation.'

36. The Denouement.
5th April 2023 (After)

Towards the bottom of Grafton Lane is a small sign-posted pathway entrance on your left that if you keep to your left again brings you up to a rustic concrete walkway. It forms a foot walk approach to the old south west facing Bowling Green Farmhouse and looks out over expansive views towards the majestic Malvern Hills. By turning your head to the right you can pick out the Woodbury and Abberley Hills. They reminded me of that day at the Point to Point. On the border of the tarmac approach road to the Farmhouse is an old small stone wall which forms a great spot for walkers to rest their legs. From this spot you can feel the winds of autumn and winter coming from the south west to plunder the flat landscape of open fields and spaces of Hereford and Worcestershire. They attack the town like marauding warriors buffeting the townsfolk. In the spring and summer the patchwork of expansive fields, copse and tree lined hedgerows, radiate and burn at the hands of the smiling sun, which warm the slopes of the distant Malverns with its plethora of visible matchbox size homes glistening like iridescent candles. The landscape is cut in two all year round by the M5 motorway snaking its moving path towards Gloucestershire before slithering all the way down to Devon and finally spitting a forked tongue full of eager holiday makers towards the coast and into Cornwall. I had watched those summer scenes play out over many years from this same spot and enjoyed the bouncing clouds playing with each other, forming and renewing in their forever floating dance.

We had approached the farm house from the Worcester Road across a disused cattle grid. Detective Inspector Chandler stared deeply into the rural idyll. The clouds did not let him down today and danced their effortless English Square.

'So Andrew, now that all the scenes have been played out and the show is over what will you do now?'

'Not so much that is going to be different Raymond' I replied. The investigation over, I had been allowed the privilege of dropping formal titles in favour of an address more suitable between friends.

THE BROMSGROVE COLLECTORS' SOCIETY

'I would expect that some friendships will change. We have all been affected by these events in some way. I think my brush with the criminal justice system has left me with a light coating of mistrust and cynicism that I think I probably needed anyway. What of you?'

'Business as usual Andrew. If anything this case has spurred my desire to put away deserving cases so that the vast majority can get on with their lives. I rest assured that my work makes society safer and that bars are the first requirement towards rehabilitation if that is the eventual aim. I leave those decisions to cleverer people than me.'

'Don't underestimate yourself Raymond. I have come to respect your cognitive ability and intelligent wit. There is a profound wisdom in you that I find attractive and compelling.'

'Well thank you. I, in turn, have found our discussions along the length of this case enlightening and supportive and I have appreciated our chats along the journey.'

That, despite my embarrassing transgression during the case, meant a lot.

'Are you confident of a conviction for both of them?' I said.

273

'I remain confident in the abilities of the crown prosecution service to convince of the need for it. The evidence is all there and I think there is a mea culpa readiness in both parties to plead guilty. Then it is up to the judge and jury to convict and sentence. All our futures lay in their hands each time they sit. Theirs is a heavy responsibility.'

'I shall watch your progress to the top of the police service. I feel sure of it. It has been a pleasure.'

Raymond did not offer a response and deflected with his reply.

'Shall we walk?'

With that we rose and strode to the right, feeling the sun on our left cheeks. Dropping down to a pathway across a field and into Grafton Lane we glanced up towards Bartholomew Bramble's cottage. I couldn't help feeling sorry that it was going to be sat empty for some time, its future unsure. We walked on talking in the tones of friends and acquaintances on topics that friends and acquaintances share.

It was a beautiful spring day. As the continuing blue sky comforted the sun and an edge of cold still rested on our faces we reached Sanders Park and took possession of a park bench looking towards the town where the spire of St Johns Church still loomed large over the skyline. I never thought I would be part of a story that it looked down upon. Holding the large take carry-out cup he had just purchased from the park café in two hands, DI Raymond Chandler took a sip of his morning coffee and exhaled a long slow breath.

As we sat a red admiral butterfly, black with broad red stripes and white spots near its forewings, bounced in the air in front of us. We were both transfixed by its effortless waltz. It meandered and floated close to me, eventually settling comfortably on my forearm sleeve. It slowly spread its wings backwards and forwards in a constant alert to danger. None came and in what seemed an eternity we sat there together in a tender moment of silent peace spellbound in each other's company while the Inspector grinned on.

'Spiritually speaking, butterflies often represent change,' he said. 'A transformation and a hope for the future.' He never ceased to surprise me. I had not seen him as a spiritual man.

'They are also thought to be a medium acting as a messenger on behalf of an angel, or spirit guide offering hope or peace.'

Despite all his short comings I thought of Max in that moment. Was he trying to ask for some sort of forgiveness for his shortcomings across from the heavens or the netherworld? I brokered my views.

'Butterflies gravitate to you if you have a kind, compassionate heart inspector; they appreciate an imaginative spirit.' I thought of Clemmie and all that we had been through. Our classic faux pas with the law and our route out of it. It had been a journey from which survival had made us stronger.

Reading my thoughts the inspector moved the conversation on.

'As we have already ventured, the court may take it's time,' he said, 'but with the written statement containing an admission of guilt I am confident this case will be prosecuted in a timely fashion. The CPS are satisfied that there is ample evidence to prosecute and it is in the public interest to do so. Let us hope for a transformation.' A satisfied pause. 'Well Andrew I will miss our discussions. I have found you an insightful, honest and reliable soul...' then adding '...for ninety-nine percent of the time.'

I appreciated the light hearted nature of the jibe. We both shared a rueful moment, each probably reflecting different emotions.

'As the case progressed I counted on you for counsel and you in the fullness of time didn't let me down.'

'Thank you Inspector. I shall not say I enjoyed it but it was certainly an experience.' I held my gaze on the spire. 'Do you think there is such a thing as sin?' I mused expansively.

'Well if you're asking me if everyone is a sinner I would say probably not. Do I think there is sin? Yes. People do bad things and as a result there is evil at work in the world but thankfully there is more light than dark to be had. I often think part of my job is to protect the light from the dark. People have the power to decide and sometimes people make poor decisions but are seldom all bad. They put themselves on a path of their own choosing and step without pause from one bad choice to the next. They lose control of their own destiny because they fail to consider the consequences of their actions. That makes them criminal in the eyes of society. They then become sinners through the judgement of their peers.'

I paused to think as two dog walkers crossed the path in front of us. They nodded and smiled and we smiled back. A little simple light across our dark conversation. He carried on with his narrative not afraid of over indulgence.

'What about people who become wrapped up in circumstances who may not be all bad. They are the honest poor. What do I mean by this? One's honour is the quality within a person to know and to do what is morally right. We all have that capacity to choose Andrew. It is driven by our conscience and separates us from the beasts. People who lack conscience have no place in society. They are driven by selfish aims for selfish purposes and they don't mind the damage they leave in their wake. I have no compunction in seeking to lock them up.'

My admiration for Detective Raymond Chandler multiplied every time I met him. The modern police service had become much maligned in the media and in many cases deservedly so. I could not help feeling whilst we had people like him in the force the world was a better place for it.

'I believe that there is evil out there Inspector and as Burke suggested, evil prospers when good men do nothing.'

'Very good Andrew, a similar sentiment but not quite right. What he actually said if you want to quote the man, and this is written and printed in his name, was *'When bad men combine, the good must associate; else they will fall, one by one, an unpitied sacrifice in a contemptable struggle.'*

'You are a gentleman and a scholar,' I said 'and I shall miss you.'

'And you sir have been an insightful guide and confident throughout. I shall miss you too. If you ever contemplate a change of career the force needs good men like you.'

I smiled. One chapter like this in my book of life was enough for me.

37. Time enough for tea.
6th April 2023 (After)

Elise Goodrich sat in her drawing room with Sangita Kumari Sangar and Balwinder Singh. They were gathered around a well-proportioned occasional table drinking Darjeeling tea from a set of Bone China Royal Stafford tea cups decorated with pale yellow and blue butterflies.

'The secret has survived it seems,' said Elise. 'Despite the interests of the constabulary the pact held strong and our foolishness has not incurred a cost.'

'You say that but this whole venture has cost me my principles, my honesty and my integrity,' bemoaned Balwinder.

'But we didn't actually do anything wrong Bal. We thought about doing something stupid but in the end we didn't. You can't say you have compromised your principles through thought, otherwise at least half the world would be in prison.' Sangita shuffled in her seat a little too pleased with her response as she looked over to Elise for approval.

'I have lied to the police,' he went on.

'Actually you haven't. You just didn't tell them everything. You told them the most important thing which were Bart's problems and his actions under duress.' Elise was her usual calm composed self. She continued,

'You only acted out of reluctant instinct. Remember what you have told us in the past; that your name in part is translated to *powerful king* and in part kings protect; that is what you sought to do. Our intentions were noble and we have nothing to be ashamed of. We were trying to support a friend, someone that we cared about and who opened up to us for help. The fact that we very nearly became involved in something that we would have come to regret is a cause of some discomfort but no one other than us needs to know.'

'It could come out in the court case,' noted Sangita.

'How? Bart doesn't know what we planned to do. He may share his story but he doesn't know the most important part that we sought to play. We are safe as long as we stick together and even if we don't we have individual plausible deniability. Nothing *actually* happened.' There was a stern note of authority in her voice as Elise looked for a reaction from the other two. There was none to worry about.

Sangita sat quietly thinking. She thought of her personal loyalty to Elise. She had provided sound advice on her crypto excursion and as a result she had recovered nearly eighty percent of her losses before cashing out. It had been a painful learning curve and her venture into unregulated currency had been a mistake that she had regretted. Elise had stood by her through the whole experience and her wisdom had shone through. She believed that Elise was right again and she owed her allegiance. Her husband would be distraught if he found out – which she vowed he never would. The fact that she served him a sleeping draught that eventful night would haunt her forever. She would pay him back with kindness for the rest of their lives and her attention would surprise him.

Balwinder would live with a little remorse for the rest of his days but accepted that they had come close to catastrophe without crossing the line to consequential action. It would never be something he was proud of but on reflection it was something that he could live with. He never divulged that he had shared their secret with me.

Elise smiled and her gentle radiance shone across the room.

'Right, anymore tea anyone?'

38. Moving on. 31ˢᵗ April 2023 (In conclusion)

It had been another beautiful day full of spring brightness. From the window of my office I could see the sun reach out touching the top of the church spire and its' rays cascaded down the steep tiles, flooding the roof of the nave. I looked on that spire differently now; spiritually, historically and figuratively. Always present, always there I thought, like an ever-watchful parent tending their offspring from above. I looked at my watch; it was time to go. I tidied my desk, gathered my bag and put on my coat, saying my goodbyes as I left the building. I knew where I was heading. The cemetery was a short walk away and I wanted to get there in the light. At the entrance Clemmie was waiting shivering slightly in the shade and waving away a curious bee that was buzzing softly around her head. 'Like bees to honey,' I thought in loving reverie.

We entered God's acre together, held a few silent moments in memory peering at Max's gravestone and headed for Area B in search of the spot under one of the monkey puzzle trees planted by the Victorians as an 'attractive ornament to the town'. Lamont and Sassy were there waiting. They had become inseparable, the thread of their story woven forever into the fabric of recent events. With Lamont's help I had won back Sassy's confidence after getting Ora involved in the sorry saga. Clemmie had always insisted it had been her fault but I think we had all shared a little blame. Anyway, whatever the route we were firm friends now.

We all quickly found what we were looking for and I felt a little nervous about what I had planned.

'In loving memory of a very dear father' we read. A pause, a brief glance at each other and then we read on.

'Anthony E. Pratt Born 10th August 1903 Died 9th April 1994 Inventor of 'Cludeo' Sadly missed.

'Well my dear Great Grandpa,' I said. 'I hope we all did you proud. It was Miss Farrier, with the needle in the car. Not quite the candlestick in the library but a little more contemporary.'

With that we all stood in silence for a minute and then with a gentle smile to each other Lamont and Sassy and Clemmie and I walked towards the park arm in arm, with our lives, our hopes and our futures.

Footnote. 14th February 2024 (After)

It took an age for the case to be heard at Crown Court but eventually, following the guilty plea at the first hearing, the Court convened to consider sentencing for both Lickey Farrier and Bartholomew Bramble. It didn't seem like the timely fashion that DI Chandler had predicted and the date of the sentencing was heavily ironic. I was there to hear the verdict and my emotions were mixed. I felt sorry for both of them yet held some enmity towards then too. They were both pathetic in their own ways and although Max had behaved appallingly, the plan that was hatched to murder him was unforgivable. Bart, as an accomplice, knowingly and voluntarily aided in the offence. Their early guilty plea did aid their sentences but mandatory minimum term sentencing for murder affected them. A twenty-year sentence with eligibility for parole after sixteen years left them stunned, their lives altered forever. The very thing that Bart had sought to avoid in his liaison with Max – a prison sentence – had come back to haunt him, whilst Lickey's moment of victorious revenge had proved a costly satisfaction. Justice had been served but Max his reputation in ruins, remained buried and all the lives of those involved changed forever.

If there was a positive to be brought out of this tragedy it was that Lickey became a cause celebre as an advocate of women in abusive relationships. The case and its outcome gained traction on social media and she was able to support the empowerment of women from behind bars. She recognised her failings and regretted her response but wanted to support others who may be in a similar position. This gave her purpose and direction and she managed it well. There was a way back, the wounds would heal and she would be a stronger woman as a result, she was sure. She was not against men, far from it but wanted others to recognise the traits that she had not. I could not help feeling slightly proud of Lickey. She had been dealt an awful hand and had played it badly. Now she was stacking her cards with aces from inside a prison cell. I often thought about her and how as a man I hadn't recognised the worst of Max. It would never happen again in my social circle.

The society had met twice since sentencing but with Max dead and Lickey and Bart behind bars the collectors were down to eight. It felt like we had all been punched in the gut and the group was reeling. It was struggling to breath and I was not sure I had the capacity to drive new life into it. It was Clemmie who scolded me on the subject. 'What happened was not because you tried to do something good Andrew. The events hovered like a satellite around your collectors but took place independently and would have happened anyway. Don't blame yourself.' I knew she was right but I needed to hear it. Thankfully, Elise stepped up as well. She said she felt some responsibility and an obligation to help re-energise the group. I didn't know what she meant but Sangita and Balwinder nodded in agreement; something that stirred a wonder in me. It also cheered me up and galvanised my metal. On wards and upwards I thought. Now, who else would be good to join our little sioree?

About the author

Steven George grew up in Leeds, West Yorkshire. He was educated at Leeds Modern Grammar School before obtaining a degree in Sports Science at Loughborough University.

He began his professional life as a teacher of Physical Education and progressed to become a long-standing Head teacher of an all-through Academy catering for four-to-eighteen-year-old pupils. After devoting forty-one years to the state education sector he is now retired and living in Worcestershire where he has at last found the time to follow his passion for writing. This is his first novel.

Steve lives with his wife Sharon and has two children and two grandchildren.

Printed in Great Britain
by Amazon